PRAISE FOR ROBYN BACHAR'S BAD WITCH SERIES

This is a wonderfully imaginative tale that begs a re-read just so that every detail and nuance can be savored.

— *RT BOOK REVIEWS*, 4 1/2 STAR REVIEW
FOR *THE IMPORTANCE OF BEING EMILY*

Blood, Smoke and Mirrors contains all the things I love the best in books, great internal and external tension, quirky or slightly flawed protagonists, great dialogue, and a captivating story line.

— *LONG AND SHORT ROMANCE REVIEWS*,
5 BOOK REVIEW

FIRE IN THE BLOOD is a sizzling, suspenseful paranormal romance.

— *FRESH FICTION*

I am seriously recommending that you read this book if you want something to distract you from anything and everything on your mind. The world painted in this book is such a great one to escape to that I literally could not put it down.

— *NIGHT OWL REVIEWS, 5* STAR TOP PICK REVIEW FOR *BEWITCHED, BLOODED AND BEWILDERED*

THE BLOODY END

Copyright © 2023 by Robyn Bachar

Editing by Mackenzie Walton

Cover by Kanaxa

Ebook ISBN: 978-1-7335761-8-5

Print ISBN: 978-1-7335761-9-2

Robyn Bachar

7301 W. 25th St.

Suite #131

North Riverside, IL 60546

THE BLOODY END

BAD WITCH BOOK 7

ROBYN BACHAR

ACKNOWLEDGMENTS

What a long, strange trip it's been. My Bad Witch journey began in 2006 when *Blood, Smoke and Mirrors* was born as my first National Novel Writing Month project. Countless people have helped me along the way on my writing journey—critique groups, RWA chapters, editors, friends and family.

Thank you to my patient readers, especially those who poked me along the way to finish *The Bloody End*. It never fails to amaze me how many people have enjoyed this series. You are all made of awesome.

A special thank you goes to my BFF Diana, who was supported my writing since *Blood, Smoke and Mirrors* was a work-in-progress and who I am grateful for every day.

But most of all, I am grateful for the love and support of my family. My parents continue to be my biggest fans, who even read the books I specifically told them not to. Thank you for always believing in me.

CONTENTS

CHAPTER ONE

Ivy

A storm was coming. For anyone else that would be foreboding, but not for me. I love storms, always have—it's almost literally in my blood, and the rush of a good storm is addicting as any drug.

"Natasha! Yelena! Time to go."

I whistled for my dogs, and they bounded away from whatever mysterious frozen find they had discovered on the beach. Their "treasures" weren't as horrifying during winter, for which I was grateful, because dead fish in January smelled less disgusting than they did in July.

Thunder rumbled on the horizon and energy zinged from my head to my toes. I rubbed my tingling arms as I eyed the approaching slate-gray clouds. There was something different about this storm. I'm no Seer, but I could tell trouble was on the way. A faint scent of ozone and a hint of copper on my tongue meant that no good would come of this. It was time to batten down the hatches.

The dogs romped up to meet me with wide Staffy-mix smile and their furry butts wriggling with joy, a sight that was made even more adorable by the custom Poison Apples sweatshirts I'd had made for them. Each one was emblazoned with our band's acid-green apple logo and proudly sported the words *My Mama's Words are Poison.*

"Come on, ladies," I said. "Let's get warmed up before dinner."

The pair barked in reply and zoomed toward the house. It's nice having a private beach where the dogs can burn off energy—well, technically the entire island is private property. A tiny pinprick of land within Lake Michigan. I'd bought the property years ago as a real estate investment and had the mansion on it renovated and restored to its former glory. Constructed during the Roaring Twenties, the building had been an eccentric mix of old-world wealthy excess and modern art deco décor, until the owner put a bullet through his brain when the stock market crashed in 1929. It changed hands a few times after that and gained a reputation of "beautiful but definitely haunted" and fell into disrepair.

Just like me. Beautiful but haunted, fallen into disrepair.

The sound of excited barking and happy whining greeted me as I made the last turn on the path back to the house. I froze as fear constricted my chest—usually the girls are only that happy when my bandmates visit (and spoil them rotten), but the guys were all West Coast babies who couldn't stand the cold, so I was sure they hadn't dropped in for a surprise visit. The few locals I'd befriended wouldn't be crazy enough to come out in weather like this, which the local news had labeled with giant words of winter storm warning, "blizzard conditions, little to no visibility, sub-zero temperatures, seek shelter."

Wary, I closed my hand around the pepper spray in my coat pocket and cursed myself for not carrying my pistol. Toting a handgun around on my lonely island had felt like the height of paranoid eccentricity, though my scars were proof that someone had truly been out to get me. Besides, the last year had taught me to love storms for a new reason—the paparazzi learned right quick that a good Michigan thunderstorm could swamp their chartered boats, if they even managed to bribe one of the local captains enough to risk braving the storm. Most of the captains who sailed the lake had too much good Midwestern sense to risk their asses (and their assets).

I drew to a confused halt at the sight waiting on my back patio. A blond man in designer sunglasses and a black cashmere coat kneeled in front of what had once been the servants' entrance to the kitchen, a door that I'd painted in Poison Apple's trademark acid green in a fuck you to the oppression of laborers. The dogs, who in theory were supposed to be part of my security measures, were showering the trespasser with kisses and demanding pets and belly rubs. Good job, security team. I felt so safe.

Said trespasser looked up at my arrival when I whistled sharply to call the dogs to my side. At least they remembered that command. Traitors. They took up their positions—one to each side of me—but instead of appearing intimidating they continued grinning at the man as he rose and dusted himself off. He smiled, and the expression hit me in the gut as recognition zinged through my veins. Now there was a smile I'd been sure I'd never see again.

Zachary Harrison. *Holy shit.*

I folded my arms and raised my defenses as the rock goddess persona of Ivy Fucking Taylor settled over me like well-worn armor. I cocked one unimpressed green eyebrow. "What step are you on?"

"Pardon?" He glanced down as though a staircase had grown beneath his feet.

Gods damn it, why did his well-cultured voice still sound like liquid sex? Best sex I'd ever had, and I was quite the erotic connoisseur. Or I used to be, before...

"What step are you on? Amends is step eight. No, wait, nine." I could swear that I saw a hint of a blush on his cheeks. Not as tan as he used to be, which was probably a good thing. Less chances of skin cancer—not that magicians could get cancer, but better safe than malignant.

"Not in rehab," he said. "Therapy, yes, but this isn't a good time to take off for a visit to rehab, which is why I'm here."

My eyes narrowed as I studied him with suspicion. "Whatever you're selling, I don't want any. Now get your ass off my property before—"

My threat was cut off by a crack of thunder and I grimaced. Damn it. Terrible timing.

"How did you get here?" I asked. "The girls would've heard a boat, and I doubt any sane helicopter pilot would've flown in this."

"I walked."

"Very funny."

The corners of his irritatingly kissable lips twitched in a wry smile. "My faerie uncle gave me a lift. I think you met him during—" Zach coughed and wisely didn't continue. "Anyway, he brought me here, but he's on call now with his new bride, banishing demons."

I swallowed the obvious question of why the fuck would a faerie be banishing demons (or why a full-blooded faerie would marry a mortal summoner). Right then.

"Before I invite you in, I want your sworn oath that you won't attempt to harm me or mine in any way."

"Of course. I swear that I will not attempt to harm you or yours in any way."

The air hummed around us as the oath set, which was as

good a guarantee as I was going to get. With a sigh I pulled my housekeys from my pocket and shooed him out of the way.

"You can stay the night—in a guest room," I added for emphasis. I unlocked the door and waved the group into the mudroom. "But you're out of here in the morning."

"It will still be storming in the morning." Zach shucked his coat and hung it on an empty hook as I divested the dogs of their sweatshirts and tossed them in a hamper.

"Not in Faerie it won't."

"You'd be surprised." The words were almost too soft to hear, and I shivered. That didn't bode well.

When everyone was free of their winter attire we headed into the kitchen. "Coffee?"

"Yes, thank you. Decaf?"

"Not in this house." I snorted. "Decaf coffee is an abomination. I've got a casserole in the oven for dinner. Should be enough for two, I planned for leftovers."

Zach seated himself at the kitchen table and studied his surroundings. The mansion's kitchen was too big for two people—to be honest, the entire place was too big for me and my girls, but after the incident I found myself with an overabundance of time on my hands during my recuperation and a new enthusiasm for household management. I polished silver and beat carpets as though preparing for a party I'd never host. It was sad and ridiculous in a gothic sort of way.

"You look well," he said.

I swallowed the reply that I looked like shit and went with "thanks" instead. Months of solitude resulted in zero fucks to give about my appearance.

"Your hair is particularly striking."

I reached up in reflex and patted the messy bun I'd twisted it into. "The green streaks were fun, but I figured I could get away with an all-over enchantment now since no one's obsessively monitoring my roots on social media."

Zach nodded and then was surprisingly quiet as I set about brewing coffee—the enormity of the room let me keep an eye on him at all times as I worked. I expected him to immediately launch into a pitch for whatever bullshit he was selling. Real estate and charities were his straight jobs, but I suspected he was here for magician reasons. Not sure why—he was an alchemist, and as far as he knew I was a sorceress of middling skill, too weak for any house or family to consider recruiting.

I set a mug in front of him, along with containers of cream and sugar, but Zach and the dogs were focused on the doorway leading to the dining room.

I straightened and addressed thin air. "This is Zach. He's a guest. Be nice to him, please."

Zach jolted. "You can see them?"

"Nope." I chose the chair across from him and added a bit of sugar to my coffee. "Can't hear them either, though we communicate through knocking when necessary."

Almost on cue, a sharp knock rapped on the doorframe—one knock for yes, two for no. Many of the previous owners and prospective buyers had scoffed at the idea of the place being haunted, but I was a magician. I knew full well that ghosts were real, but only necromancers could see and communicate with them.

My train of thought screeched to a halt, and I pressed both palms flat on the tabletop as I fought a surge of panic. Six years was a long time, and it was definitely long enough for a magician to begin studying necromancy. Magicians are born with different flavors of inherent magic, but necromancy was a field that any magician could choose to study. A gross, disgusting field that featured tricks like enslaving ghosts, raising zombies, and, if the student was lucky, graduating to immortality as a master necromancer.

I swallowed hard as my heart pounded in my chest. "You're a necromancer now?"

"I am."

Zach raised both hands in surrender and held them still. He'd left his sunglasses in his coat, and his pretty green eyes seemed sincere enough. My fingers itched to trace the scars on my throat that had been left behind by the last necromancer I'd encountered—the master necro who'd stalked and tried to kill me. I flinched at the memory as phantom pain squeezed my windpipe. I tried to console myself with the fact that the dogs liked Zach. They were good judges of character —since adopting them I'd become a believer in a dog's ability to sense people's intentions. If my dogs didn't like you, then I didn't like you, either.

"And in the spirit of full disclosure," he said. "I'm not an apprentice. I'm a master necromancer.

Holy shit. Not an idiot apprentice who'd been lured in by the promise of immortality. No, a master necro meant I'd let a full-fledged vampire into my home, but in my defense master necros weren't supposed to be able to withstand sunlight and despite the stormy weather it was absolutely afternoon outside. What the fuck?

"But I give you my oath that you are safe from me," he said. "I fed from my apprentice before I left to prevent even the slightest temptation. I would never hurt you, and I would never bite you without your express consent. I don't wish to add to your pain."

I focused on my breathing for a solid minute to calm my racing pulse—I'd known Zach, in the Biblical sense, when he was just an alchemist. A handsome, billionaire playboy alchemist who brewed all the best party drugs. I'd really liked him, too, and once upon a time I'd wanted more than our one-weekend-stand from him. I doubted that he'd come here to harm me, but that didn't mean I trusted him.

"What do you want?" My voice was almost entirely calm—score one for Team Ivy.

"I'm here for two reasons." He folded his hands in his lap, a sign of trust in much of magician society—no hand waving, no spell casting. "First, you're in danger, and I came to warn you and offer you my aid, and the aid of the pan-magician council. Second, you're my soul mate."

CHAPTER TWO

Ivy

Well, shit.

Now I kind of wished I was a Seer because I'd be able to check that statement for bullshit, but really, who lies about that? Straights, maybe. The non-magical majority could wax poetic about finding one's soul mate all they wanted, but magicians knew that soul mates were a real thing. Not that I'd ever met someone with a soul mate, mind you, but that didn't mean they weren't real. Wolfie swore up and down that were-kangaroos were a thing, and because he was a shifter himself, I was willing to give him the benefit of the doubt.

My soul mate was a vampire. Fucking hell.

Grimacing, I rose and glared down at him. "You, sir, are an asshole." I walked away to check on the casserole, even though it needed another half hour to bake.

"I'm aware."

"Are you? Are you *really?*" I paused in front of my fridge. Did I have salad fixings left? Fresh produce was hard to come by in winter, considering I lived on an island in the middle of nowhere and the lake was doing its damnedest to freeze along the shorelines.

Zach cleared his throat. "I did intend to contact you, after... Things just got busy, not to mention complicated. You know how it is."

"Bullshit." I opened the fridge, reached in and grabbed a bunch of only slightly wilted celery, which I then pointed in Zach's direction to emphasize my point. "I called you. Not once, not twice, but three times, and I *never* bother that much after sexy fun times. I made an effort and you ghosted me."

"I'm...honored?" Zach's brow furrowed, and I was quietly impressed that he hadn't gone for Botox. Then again, when men aged the media called them distinguished, while women apparently became shrill, dried-up horrors, especially when they refused to cloister themselves like proper old hags and allow nubile youngsters to have the limelight. As a musician I was well past pop-star age, but as long as I could sing, play the guitar, and write songs, I'd get along as an aging rocker.

Well, two out of three ain't bad.

"I don't remember receiving any messages from you," Zach said.

I rinsed the celery and placed it on the cutting board. For a moment I pondered asking him if he had any crudité preferences, but then I remembered that as a vampire he didn't need to eat human food—just humans, though technically only the magic in magician blood could sustain a vampire. Ah, the fun facts one learns when you had a vampire stalker trying to murder you.

Ants on a log it was then.

"I don't doubt that." I snorted and went looking for the peanut butter. I stocked up on canned, jarred, and other somewhat non-perishable goods in October after being warned to never underestimate a Michigan winter. "After the second message your secretary answered the third time and informed me that 'Mr. Harrison thanks you for the lovely time but does not wish further contact.'"

"What?" He rose, appearing indignant. "Melanie would never, and she doesn't have access to my personal phone, only my business numbers."

I scrunched my nose. "That wasn't her name. It was an L-name. Lily, or Lauren..."

"Laura?"

"Yeah, sounds right." Appropriately bland but bitchy at the same time.

Zach cursed in a language that wasn't English or the basic Latin I'd learned for sorcery purposes. Sorcerers had a stick up their asses when it came to rituals. They gave witches shit for their Seussical rhyming spells but were just as addicted to chanting dead languages. Thankfully I was spared from participating in elaborate group rituals because I wasn't a member of one of the sorcerer houses or societies.

"Problem?" I asked.

"Several." He leaned against the counter next to me and scrubbed his face with his hands. "Laura was my mentor. I didn't know it at the time, but she placed some sort of modi-fied summoner control spell on me. She wanted me for my money and fame, like I was some sort of prize to add to her collection."

"Undead gold digger, lovely." I chopped celery into log-appropriate portions. "So, you're saying that you didn't mean to ghost me, your vampire boss was just screening your calls."

"Essentially." He ran a hand through his hair. "I recently learned that the spell splintered when I became a master necromancer, and things spiraled from there, hence the therapy I'm in now. I did...terrible things."

I glanced at him, unimpressed. "The devil made you do it?"

"A devil of my own making." He tucked his hands into the pockets of his black jeans—how did I not notice those tight, tailored jeans earlier? Lord and Lady. I said a quick thank you to the denim gods.

"Aha. That's why you're on the apology tour."

Zach laughed, but it was a tired, brittle sound. "It would be a world-wide tour. I don't expect anything from you, much less forgiveness. I'm here to keep you safe."

"From what?"

"Hunters."

I paused. "What hunters?"

His brow rose. "I take it you've been out of the loop on magician news?"

I waved a hand at the kitchen. "I've been holed up in a haunted mansion on an island in Lake Michigan, what do you think?"

"Point taken," Zach said. "The short version is that a group of government hunters called Task Force Prometheus was ostensibly hunting magicians to find a biological source for magic, one the voids could exploit. They abducted my apprentice, Anthony, and after we rescued him we discovered that the group had been infiltrated by demons with their own world-ending agenda. They've been slaughtering summoners and other magicians as part of their plan to invade our world and take over."

My appetite vanished and I set my knife down. "You're shitting me."

"I wish that I were. We have a single summoner left in this territory. No one's been able to contact the West Coast, Las Vegas, and New York summoner communities. They're all presumed dead."

The enormity of that... I stood numb for a moment before my brain caught up and reminded me that Jorge, our bass guitarist, was a summoner. I cursed and grabbed my phone out of my back pocket—no signal thanks to the storm, not that cell reception is good on my tiny island. The Wi-Fi bars had also vanished.

"No, no, no. Dammit!" I bolted to my office to check if everything was down, followed by two stampeding Staffy mixes and an unfairly attractive vampire who was apparently my soul mate. I wasn't sure I believed in soul mates, but I had to admit, it was a pity I couldn't put that into a song. Then again, considering there was an impending demon invasion there might not be time for new songs.

I dove into my desk chair and slapped the keyboard to wake my computer, and lo and behold, no internet connection. I scowled and turned to Zach. "Does your phone work?"

He withdrew his phone from his pocket and then shook his head. "Apparently not. Why?"

"Jorge. I have to warn him."

"The Titania is warning the members of your band."

"Which Titania?"

"The Midwestern Titania, Catherine Duquesne."

"Okay. That's good, I guess."

I didn't follow faerie-blooded politics. It was very likely that I had faerie blood, but my family had lost contact with our faerie relatives generations ago. I had enough stress in my life without digging up that information. Paz was some variety of faerie blooded, so I heard the latest Oberon and Titania drama from him. The Midwestern pair, Lex and Catherine Duquesne, were new to the Titania and Oberon scene, but that wasn't how I'd first heard of Lex Duquesne.

No, I'd learned about Lex because he'd been Nick's best friend. And I got Nick killed.

I shivered and rubbed my arms. "Why the others, though? Paz is the only one with faerie blood."

"Because along with myself, Poison Apples rounds out the top five most wanted on the hunters' list."

"We're hunter enemies two through five? What did we do?"

"I don't know. Our best guess is that your fame makes you high-profile targets. I've been poking the hunters with a pointy stick, as the Titania likes to say, so I've more than earned my spot."

"Number one with a bullet, got it." Damn it all to hells, this day just kept getting worse. "So now that I know, what? Your faerie uncle picks you up after his shift ends and you go home?"

"I'd like you to come with me."

"And abandon my fortress of solitude? I'd see hunters coming a mile away with my security system. It's armed for British tabloid paparazzi."

"But not demons."

"True, but I can add wards now that I know they're a possibility." Honestly, I hadn't really put up any wards at all. My problems were of the "mortal with a camera" variety. I'd been hyper vigilant about warding against vampires the first few months after I moved in, but it felt like a waste of time. My problem hadn't been with vampires as a whole, it'd been with one asshole stalker. Plus I didn't need some industrious Brit with a camera filming me wandering around my island performing rituals under the full moon.

Zach opened his mouth to argue, but instead he took a deep breath and walked away to flop into one of the over-stuffed reading chairs in my office. "It's bad, Ivy. Are you familiar with the Order of St. Jerome?"

My brow furrowed as I put my desktop back to sleep and

turned to give him my full attention. As a sorceress, I was familiar with several houses, families, societies and whatnot that sorcerers group themselves into to show how important they were. Keeping track of them is tiring, and since sorcerer society considers me too weak and too famous to be of use to whatever nefarious plans they're up to, I don't have to.

"No, that one's new to me," I said. "Most sorcerers won't let me play in their sandboxes."

"It's not a sorcerer society. It's a librarian one—specifically one made up of..." Zach paused for a moment, looking as though he'd swallowed an entire lemon. "Vampires, but they're not beholden to the necromancer council. They call themselves chroniclers because they're meant to chronicle magician history."

Huh. Sounded like a breed of vampire I might actually like. "Just historical events? Or artwork too? I'd love to get a look at magician musical history. Find out if anyone's studied the effects of using music in rituals."

He blinked in surprise. "I...have no idea. My point was that the hunters discovered two of the Chicago area libraries and burned them down, even kidnapped the youngest local chronicler. We had to attack their base to retrieve him."

I jumped up. "Goose-stepping fascists! I hope you burned their shit to the ground."

"We did, more or less. Our strike team included a few fire faeries." He rose and approached me, but he hesitated just out of arm's reach. "The hunters broke through wards crafted to keep out an angry mob. They know who you are, and *where* you are. They won't hesitate to abduct you, or even kill you. Please let me help you."

Damn it. I gave in to the urge to fidget with my scars—yup, still there. Phantom pains slashed my throat with teeth and claws and anxiety squeezed my lungs. I leaned against my desk as my knees wobbled. If one asshole vampire could do this to me, a demon-led posse of hunters would absolutely fuck my shit up. I'd cheated death once. Twice would be pressing my luck.

My panic spiked at the realization that I'd have to leave the mansion. My Fortress of Solitude. Demons might be able to get me here, but worse things lurked out there. Things with long lenses, bright lights and microphones that shouted endless questions.

"Ivy, were you in love with your bodyguard?"

"Ivy, will you ever sing again?"

"Ivy, show us your scars!"

I swallowed hard and exhaled a shaky breath. "This is a lot to process. I need to sleep on it. They're not likely to attack tonight, right?"

"I can't be certain, but probably not in this storm. The voids they control shouldn't be able to travel in this weather."

"Great. Let's have dinner and you can tell me the whole story from the beginning."

~

Zach

Dinner was surprisingly lovely. When I arrived uninvited I entirely expected to be set on fire and cursed within an inch of my life, but Ivy had been civil. Perhaps that was even worse than being attacked on the spot—she put on a brave front, but on occasion her words would trail off and her eyes unfocused, and it was clear she was reliving a terrible trauma.

I knew of the attack—nearly everyone in the magician community did. Though their music didn't appeal to the entire community, the members of Poison Apples were highly regarded for their success in staying hidden while moving among the voids. I'd been fighting the influence of Laura's control spell at the time, and I barely noted that Ivy was the victim in the attack. Instead, as a member of the necromancer council, I focused on damage control. Necromancers weren't liked by other magicians as a rule, and having one of ours murder a guardian and tear the throat out of a beloved musician did an enormous amount of damage to our already poor reputation.

I fluffed the pillows of the guest bed and pondered ways I could convince Ivy to leave with me in the morning. She wasn't safe here. Of course, none of us were safe anywhere with the task force and its demon masters gaining power and momentum each day. I perched on the edge of the mattress to untie my shoes. I hadn't brought any clothes or toiletries, expecting to either be evicted from the premises or leaving promptly, but Ivy's guest room was rather well stocked. She had raided her "merch room", where an assortment of the band's souvenirs was stored in stacks of cardboard boxes. With a smirk she'd presented me with a Poison Apples hooded sweatshirt and matching sweatpants to wear as pajamas. I wondered what Catherine would say if she saw me bedecked in fan attire. I should take a photo to send after the storm passed.

Ivy's pair of resident ghosts arrived to interrupt my train of thought and continue their silent disapproval. Sighing, I set my shoes aside and gave them my full attention. I'd been ignoring them since they first arrived in the kitchen—they hadn't said anything thus far, at least not to me, but I overheard them whispering to each other. I assumed they weren't the ghosts of magicians, because any magician spirit would know better than to willingly make themselves known to a necromancer.

Both ghosts were dressed in the attire of new wealth in the 1920s and appeared to have died young—well, younger than myself at least. I physically appeared the same as I did when I became a master necromancer in my late thirties. I nicknamed them Jordan and Jay. If they were smart, they wouldn't give me their real names. A necromancer could do much damage with a spirit's True Name.

"Well?" I prompted.

The woman, Jordan, narrowed her eyes. "Well what?"

She was dressed in flapper attire, the once vibrant colors of her beaded gown faded and translucent, and the garment's trademark fringed hem silently swayed in a ghostly breeze. Her dark hair was cut short in a bob that was scandalous for the time, and her painted lips were turned down in a scowl.

"You look like you have something to say, so say it," I prompted.

"How can you see us?" Jay asked. This ghost was fair-haired and handsome, and he was dressed in a light linen suit worthy of his Gatsby nicknamesake, as though he was ready to play croquet or go sailing.

The question confirmed that they were indeed spirits of voids. It was fortunate for them that I was now firmly on the path toward redemption while I came to terms with the enormity of the damage I'd caused in the last six years. If nothing else, it did prove that nothing good came from attempting to mind control another person. My mentor had learned that the hard (and fatal) way.

"You are aware that Miss Taylor possesses special abilities?" I asked, and they nodded. "One of my abilities allows me to interact with the dead. And know this, if any of you decide to run up and down the halls at three in the morning, I will, as my step-aunt says, put you in time out."

Jordan folded her arms. "We like Ivy. She's the only person

who has treated us like people and not some roadside freak show. She's been through enough, and she doesn't need you adding to her nightmares."

"I don't intend to."

Jay snorted. "The path to hell is lined with good intentions. Believe me, we should know."

I tilted my head and studied them. Would Ivy want me to release them? Some spirits stayed behind after death because they were confused and hadn't quite accepted the fact that they were dead, while others stayed because they didn't believe they had earned the right to move on. Those were the ones who evolved into cranky bastards who stomped around at night.

"I'm aware. I'm here to help her, not harm her." And I had a group of somewhat well-meaning allies who were watching me like proverbial hawks, waiting for me to revert to my previous bad behavior so that they could put me in time out, with extreme prejudice. I tried, repeatedly, to apologize to Catherine for my terrible behavior. My gut twisted at the thought—it was a peculiar holdover from mortal life that while I didn't need to eat solid food, I could still feel nauseous. Looking back at my life with Laura and the way I'd behaved...

The easy way out would be to declare that I only did those things because I was under the effects of Laura's shattered mind control spell, but it would be a lie. I behaved like a monster because the potential had been within me all the time, in my blood and bone, thanks to my shadowspawn faerie mother. She was the pinnacle of selfish behavior, a force of nature who left destruction and chaos in her wake. My father called her Hurricane Helen, and he hadn't been wrong.

It had taken so little to unleash my inner monster. I wanted to be a better man, and I had repeatedly promised

Anne, the seer who had discovered my soul mate's identity, that I would be on my best behavior with Ivy. I'd caused so much destruction when I lived under Laura's influence, and now that I'd been granted a second chance I intended to do everything within my power to become a hero, not a villain.

I straightened and smiled. "Is there something I can do for you? You don't have to stay here."

The spirits looked at each other, clearly surprised by the offer.

"Where would we go?" Jay asked.

"You have a few options. I can release you from your ties to this house, and you can move on to what lies beyond."

"To heaven?" Jordan's dark eyes widened.

I chuckled. "I'm no priest, so I couldn't tell you for certain. Popular magician belief says that we move on, reflect on what we learned in our previous life, and then continue to a new one."

Which, of course, meant that vampires were in breach of contract with the higher powers. We died but didn't move on or become spirits. Catherine had referred to it as "putting a spike in the wheel of life", because witches are prone to melodrama.

"What are the other options?" Jordan asked.

"I could bind you to an object, like a ring or a locket, which would allow you to travel with Miss Taylor."

Jordan perked up at that. "We could go on tour with her?"

"She can't sing in public again," Jay said.

Jordan elbowed him and the feather plume in her head-band bobbed with the motion. "Don't tell him that! It's not his business."

I held up hands to calm them. "I need to speak with Ivy to ensure she's all right with that option if you want to pursue it. You can also simply stay here, but I don't recommend it, because the hunters will eventually arrive looking for her, and when they do, their demon commanders will not be as... pleasant to you as I am."

The spirits were visibly distraught at that idea, and I didn't blame them. For all the terrible things I'd done, they still paled in comparison to what a demon could do to an innocent soul.

"Think about it, and we'll discuss with Ivy in the morning, all right?"

"Square deal," Jordan said. "Sleep well."

They vanished, and I flopped back on the bed for a moment of wallowing. *Laura had answered my phone. Laura chased away Ivy—my soul mate.* Damn it all. A miserable part of me accepted that I deserved it—the part that had grown stronger each time my parents rejected me. I was always too human for my mother and too freakish for my void father. Faust was the only one who ever accepted me as-is, and how did I thank him? I tried to kill his soul mate. Though, to be honest, Patience Roberts and I had always gotten along like oil and water. I might've tried to kill her even if I hadn't blamed her for aiding Catherine in breaking our bond.

You don't deserve a second chance.

Probably not.

Who do you think you are, playing at being a hero?

Why did my sneering inner voice sound so much like my mother? If this kept up I was one rundown motel away from becoming Norman Bates.

I'd already gone through my own Jay Gatsby phase—an undead, unstable Jay Gatsby, who had kidnapped and bound my Daisy Buchanan to me with magic rather than gaze at her from afar. For a moment I indulged in the image of Alexander Duquesne as a brutish Tom Buchanan, but that sort of petty thinking was part of the behavior I was attempting to rise above—slowly, like a ponderous Hindenburg about to crash and burn at any moment. There were a startling number of people who thought I didn't deserve a chance for redemption—myself included. Hindsight was 20/20, and my past was a minefield of unforgivable behavior.

I shook my head and decided to drown the self-disgust with a hot shower and the dubious comfort of my new pajamas. In theory, things would look brighter in the morning.

Of course, that moment the storm decided to remind me of its presence with a boom of thunder that rattled the house.

None of this boded well.

CHAPTER THREE

Ivy

Yeah, Zach might deny it, but he was definitely walking the rehab path.

On any other day his attempts to make amends would've been cute considering how unusually attentive he was—aside from his obligatory charity work, concern for the welfare of others wasn't on-brand for Zach Harrison. He'd even tried, and more or less succeeded, at making breakfast, depending on how you felt about blackened toast and crunchy scrambled eggs. As a kid who'd grown up in poverty, I never turned down food, because I remembered all too well the hunger pangs when we didn't have enough to go around. It was part of the reason why I supported so many children's support groups—I had a rotten childhood, and now I had more than enough money to spread around to help kids growing up like I did.

But this wasn't any other day, and with the storm howling around my haunted mansion I was about to vibrate out of my skin with excess energy. I almost wished the hunters would show up because I could literally bring down the thunder on them right now.

"Are you okay?" Zach asked for the fourth time.

I set my fork down and scowled. "I am many things. Okay is not one of them. Everything is more than a little fucked up right now."

"Point taken."

I leaned back in my chair and folded my arms. "What are you looking for with this soul mate thing? I always thought soul mates were a faerie story. Like soul mates went extinct with the elves, or that they were one of those, 'if it sounds too good to be true, it probably is' kind of things."

"And you an artist? How unpoetic of you." The corners of his mouth twitched with amusement and I rolled my eyes.

"The universe is infinite, and two people just happen to share the halves of the same soul? And they somehow find each other and live happily ever after? Not likely."

"Says the sorceress who fronts an all-magician band. Through magic, all things are possible."

I narrowed my eyes—pretty sure he'd stolen that line from *Star Wars*. "Uh huh."

"You are correct that soul mates aren't always a romantic match, or guaranteed happiness. According to my *librarian cousin*," Zach spoke the words as though they left a foul taste in his mouth, "some matches are platonic, like best friends. But I assumed that our match was romantic due to the evidence of our obvious chemistry."

I rolled my eyes at the near-pun—Zach had been an alchemist when we met, and he'd had all the best party potions. The weekend we spent together had been spectacular. That just proved that we were physically compatible, but not emotionally so. I sighed and rubbed at my eyes as the ghosts of hangovers past hammered through my skull.

Depending on the promises made by the particular rehab program, sobriety was supposed to be some sort of happy, glowing state where you'd conquered your inner addiction demons, survived all your lowest lows, and come out stronger for it. So far, stronger hadn't been all it was cracked up to be. I'd replaced the addiction demons with anxiety, self-doubt, grief, and regret.

I knew how it felt to have a loved one die to protect you, starting with my mother, then Nick, and now what? Zach was going to shield me from a demon horde? My stomach twisted and I swallowed hard. I should tell him. I'd tortured myself over the last few months with the question of whether Nick would have survived if I'd entrusted him with my truth.

"How did you find out about us?" I asked.

"From a seer. She promised to find my soul mate in exchange for..."

"Magic beans?" I guessed. He winced and it triggered my bullshit alarm. "In exchange for what?"

Zach cleared his throat. "I wasn't quite in my right mind at the time due to a spell gone wrong. Unfortunately, I threatened her for the information."

My eyes narrowed—threats from vampires were definitely in my top five least favorite things. Zach seemed to realize this and raised his hands in surrender.

"We are on speaking terms now. The seer and her soul mate are both part of the pan-magician council." He grimaced. "And, as it turns out, her soul mate is my librarian cousin."

Before we could continue, the empty egg carton slid off the kitchen counter and toppled to the floor. I quirked an eyebrow at Zach, who sighed. "Your resident ghosts want to speak with you."

"And you can make that happen?" Other than drinking

magician blood, I wasn't entirely sure what master necromancers did with their immortality. Have goth parties where they debated whose cape was the coolest?

"I can, if you're willing."

Huh. Not gonna lie, it sounded interesting. "What do you need me to do?"

"Give me your hand, and I'll cast the spell that will allow you to see and hear them for a limited time."

Hand holding seemed mild enough, and I could always stab him with my fork if things soured. I gave him my hand, and after some muttering in Latin (why Latin, was it a Western magician thing?) two ghosts appeared in my kitchen. A shockingly average man and woman who looked to be in their twenties—no bloody wounds or corpse-like skin—were dressed for a cocktail party in the 1920s. The ghosts appeared faded, like an old photo left too long in the sun. Zach gave my hand a gentle squeeze before releasing me.

"There's two of you?" Color me surprised—I suspected that there was more than one spirit in residence, but I'd been envisioning anywhere up to a dozen from the racket they made when experiencing a ghostly tantrum.

The flapper nodded. "Yeah, and we think you're the bee's knees! I'm—"

"Please don't," Zach said. "Remember, it's better if I don't know your real names." He turned to me. "I've been mentally referring to them as Jordan and Jay."

After a moment I recognized the reference—Jordan Baker and Jay Gatsby—and I snickered. "I'm surprised that you're a fan of fiction."

He smiled dryly. "That particular book should be required reading for wealthy playboys. A cautionary tale."

"How wealthy?" Jordan asked.

"Never you mind," I said. "What did you want to ask?"

Jay straightened. "May we accompany you when you leave? Your...friend explained that he could perform some sort of magic that would allow us to go where you go."

"And that it might be dangerous if we stay behind," Jordan said.

I turned to Zach. "Dangerous how?"

"The mortal hunters wouldn't pose a problem. The demons, on the other hand, would see your ghostly house-mates, and that..."

"Would be bad, right." I turned to my resident grim grinning ghosts. Would they be considered hitchhiking ghosts if Zach somehow bound them to me? My own Greek choir to follow me around and comment on my poor life choices.

"The other option," Zach said, "would be to release their ties to this place so that they can move on."

"And you're not excited about that option?" I asked the ghosts.

"I want to go on tour!" Jordan bounced in place and the beaded fringe of her dress swayed with the enthusiastic motion.

I stroked my throat as I shoved down a surge of fear. My speaking voice functioned decently, but my singing voice hadn't recovered enough to survive a worldwide stadium tour, or even a domestic dive bar tour. My Ivy Fucking Taylor façade had seen me through many a PR disaster, but this...I wasn't sure if I had the strength to face the media mob.

"I won't be going on tour for the foreseeable future," I informed Jordan, "especially if the apocalypse is approaching. But if you won't be safe here, and you're not ready to move on, then yeah, it's best that you come with us."

"You're agreeing to leave?" Zach asked me.

My lips pressed in a grim line as I considered my reply. Did I want to leave? Fuck no. I wasn't finished healing—

mentally, physically, or emotionally. Life on my tiny island was calm, peaceful and safe in ways I'd hadn't experienced since... probably ever, come to think of it. My life had gone from the series of unfortunate events of my youth to the series of super fun but definitely dangerous in myriad ways events of my music career. My weekend in Vegas with Zach hadn't been my first sex, drugs, and rock-and-roll rodeo of debauchery, and it hadn't been my last.

No, my last rodeo had been with Nick, and it ended with two dead and a gaping wound in my neck. Not the best party ever. Zero stars, do not recommend.

Unless Zach was selling a big bag of bullshit with his end of the world story, I should retreat to somewhere with proper wards and magical defenses. Tasers and pepper spray weren't going to deter demons. Blessed pepper spray? I filed that idea away for later.

The real whopper of a question was, would Zach be safe with me? All recent signs pointed to no. If a guardian couldn't protect me from a vampire stalker, what was Zach going to do against a demon army? Flash his pretty playboy smile (now upgraded with fangs) and offer them a real estate deal? Considering my run of rotten luck, maybe Zach should be looking for protection *from* me, instead of *for* me.

Thunder crashed and lightning struck nearby, and power surged beneath my skin like a rush of adrenaline. I tried to shunt the magic away, but the attempt made the electricity in the house surge and shut off. I cursed under my breath and rose.

"We've blown a fuse." I dusted my hands on the legs of my jeans to hide the slight scorch marks on my fingertips. "I'll go down and fix it."

"I'll come with you," Zach said.

"Do you know anything about fuse boxes as old as, well, them?" I motioned to the ghosts.

"No, but I can provide moral support." Zach grinned, and I snorted.

"Have it your way." I grabbed two flashlights from the cabinet closest to the mud room, and then led him to the cellar.

"You didn't upgrade the electrical when you remodeled?" Zach asked as we navigated the treacherous wooden stairs.

"Restore, not remodel," I corrected. "We did a lot of rewiring and everything's up to code now. We focused on repair for original fixtures that could be salvaged and upgraded the things that couldn't. Old girl needed a facelift, not a total body makeover."

"And we thank you for that," Jay said. Apparently the ghosts were joining us on our expedition to the depths of the basement.

"It still feels like home," Jordan said.

I fought down a sigh—they shouldn't have to leave the mansion. Just one more tick of bad karma on my permanent record. Some days I wondered if I'd created a self-fulfilling prophecy when I'd developed my stage persona. My words really were poison, and they infected everything and everyone around me.

Like your soul mate?

Scowling, I followed the flashlight's beam as I slowly made my way through the collection of antiques awaiting restoration. The ghosts chatted about the history of the different pieces until I reached the fuse box.

Zach peered over my shoulder. "That looks like a fire hazard."

"Not anymore. It's one hundred percent building inspector approved." I grimaced at the blown fuses—apparently my magical mishap had fried all of them. I pulled old fuses and set them aside, then searched for the box of new ones that I knew was kept nearby. Somewhere.

"A new system—" Zach began, but I cut him off.

"Yeah, yeah. I'm sure you would've paved the place and put up a parking lot. For a vamp—ahem, necromancer you should have a greater appreciation for the history of things."

"And this house has an interesting history," Jay said. "We're buried down here."

"*What?*" I fumbled the box of fuses and turned toward his voice, and then I swallowed a yelp. The spirits had faded further to wispy outlines filled with an otherworldly mist.

"Really?" Zach asked. I disliked the curious note in his voice and I glared at him.

"Hey, you're not allowed to raise my housemates as zombies, or skeletal minions, or whatever devious plan you're hatching."

"It would make the binding spell easier if I had a piece of each of them." Zach tilted his head in the faint glow of our flashlights.

I swallowed the bile that bolted up at the thought of acquiring "pieces" of Jordan and Jay's bodies. Worse, of carrying the things around. Would the spell create a ghoulish bone necklace? A locket filled with decomposing hair? A bracelet of teeth? I cursed my imagination and took several deep breaths to banish the nausea before continuing, and I pointedly ignored Zach's conversation with the ghosts as I worked.

Power restored, I turned and discovered that I couldn't see the ghosts, and the only hint of their presence was the disembodied whisper of their voices.

"Okay, I'm going to find somewhere to hide while you work. Find me when you're ready."

"You're saying yes?" Jordan's voice whispered behind me and I squeaked in surprise. Oh for fuck's sake, I'd been through way worse, ghosts should hardly ping my fear radar.

I sighed and nodded. "We all need to bunker down somewhere safer until the crisis is averted or the world ends, whichever happens first."

"I appreciate your faith in my abilities," Zach said dryly.

"Oh, I didn't know that you're single-handedly cancelling this apocalypse." I squinted at him. "You're going to, what? Fly a magic nuke into demon space, Tony Stark?"

"The council is developing a plan."

"Great, I feel so much safer now." I waved a hand. "Leaving. Happy haunting, or whatever this entails. Don't tell me. Ignorance of necromancy is bliss."

~

Zach

Ritual completed, I returned to my guest room to wash the grave dirt from my hands. Ivy had likely been right to leave—few people had the intestinal fortitude for witnessing necromancy rituals—but the resident ghosts were no longer bound to the house they haunted, and instead were connected to Jordan's necklace. Jordan had pragmatically warned me not to tell Ivy where I'd found the necklace, other than to say "the cellar", though even I was aware of the fact that few people would be willing to wear jewelry that someone had been violently murdered in. Apparently their killer had attacked them with a hatchet, buried the bodies and covered up the crime thanks to the convenient circumstance of the stock market crash that happened the next day.

Very unpleasant.

Once I was presentable, I went in search of Ivy. My ghostly guides had disappeared for some rest, or whatever it was that ghosts did when they weren't wandering about in eternal melancholy. The house was quiet except for the storm continuing to batter the walls. I checked my phone again—still no signal. I could call for my faerie relatives if an emergency arose, but considering that Faust and his ever-irritating bride were on banishing duty, I didn't want to interrupt until their shift ended. And if the worst occurred and my uncle couldn't reach me, there was always the very last resort of calling my mother. Fair Helen, as Faust referred to her, caused havoc everywhere she went, and her presence here would only slightly preferable to a demon attack. Keeping my mother at bay was possibly the only positive thing that Laura had done for me.

I turned a corner and followed the sound of a piano being played. The door to the music room had been left ajar, probably so I could locate Ivy after having performed my ritual. The melody wasn't familiar. One of the first things I'd done after realizing that Ivy was my soul mate was to reacquaint myself with Poison Apples' music. The band had evolved from its punk-pop "parents don't understand" beginnings to a more socially conscious rage against inequality, particularly targeting old money and greedy businessmen.

Like you.

I bit back a sigh and reached to knock on the doorframe to announce my presence, but I froze as Ivy began to sing. Awestruck, I watched from the doorway and hung on every word of her new song. All reports from the non-magician media agreed that Ivy would never sing again due to the trauma to her throat, and the scars she carried seemed to reinforce that claim. It was tragic, because the fame she'd earned among the voids had also prevented her from allowing a witch to properly heal the wounds left by her stalker. Phantom bile rose in my throat—I'd been a hairsbreadth away from devolving into the same reckless obsession displayed by the master who attacked Ivy.

Perhaps she'd received just enough healing to her vocal cords to allow her to perform again. Her singing voice had changed, or it could be the softer subject matter. Ivy was known for her ability to blast the audience with her lyrics in perfect, furious pitch, but now her voice was softer, smokier —the broken croon of a blues singer lamenting a lost love. My brow furrowed as I pondered the subject of the song, and then rage sizzled like fire through my veins. Ivy was singing about Nick Bruno, the guardian who had died protecting her. I clenched my fists at the thought that Ivy was in love with a guardian, just like the previous object of my affection, Catherine. The idea that my own soul mate could also be in love with someone else—a guardian, no less—was intolerable.

Oh yeah, you've changed. A real portrait of self control.

Damn it all. That mocking voice of reason sounded too much like Catherine. I forced the anger away and focused on taking several calming breaths. There was no point in repeating past mistakes. I was supposed to be better than this now that I was free of Laura's spell.

Unless you were always like this. A spoiled, entitled brat incapable of caring for the welfare of others.

Entirely possible. I didn't have positive role models as a child—a shadowspawn faerie for a mother and a Wall Street robber baron for a father. Shallow, spiteful people who only cared about appearances. My chest tightened with anxiety as I listened to my soul mate pour out her feelings for the fallen hero who had loved and died for her, and who was, undoubtedly, a better man than I.

I gathered what little composure I had left and knocked

Ivy startled and her fingers hit a discordant note on the keys. She turned and sat sideways on the bench to watch my approach as I entered the room.

"Planning a new album?" I asked politely.

She shrugged. "The boys are getting antsy, and our manager might lose his mind if I don't give him good news soon."

"Is it? Good news?"

Ivy opened her mouth to reply, but then frowned. "For him, sure. I'm not ready to be out in the world again. The exterior scars healed a lot faster than my mental ones. I get nightmares. Flashbacks."

"Is there anything I can do?" It seemed the thing to say, through to be honest I had no idea how to help her mourn or recover.

"Stop being a vampire?" Ivy blurted, and I flinched. Her eyes widened and she clapped a hand over her mouth with a mortified expression, but the damage had already been done, like a knife to my undead heart. "Shit! I'm sorry, I didn't mean that."

I nodded and swallowed hard—she might not have meant to say them aloud, but she meant those words. We couldn't be more ill-suited to each other, though once upon a time we would've been perfect. A Hollywood power couple, a magical force to be reckoned with.

But I'd been afraid of pursuing a relationship, and then Laura swooped in to distract me from my soul mate and lead me down a darker path than I'd ever intended to walk.

I did this. These were my consequences.

I cleared my throat. "The ritual is over. Your housemates are bound to this necklace." I withdrew the jewelry in question from my pocket, a black and silver art-deco piece comprised of slender geometric shapes. I'd cleaned it as best I could in the guest room sink, but it needed a proper cleaning to restore its shine. I crossed to Ivy and she took it, eyeing the piece speculatively.

"It's not really my style. Do I have to wear it? Or just have it near me?"

"Near should suffice. You can always put it in your pocket, perhaps in a pouch to keep it safe. The spell will end if the chain breaks."

"What happens then? Will the ghosts be okay?"

"They'll be untethered. It's a bad state for a ghost to be in." I paused and glanced around the room—the decor was a mix of soft pink furniture surrounded by angular black and gold fixtures and the ebony grand piano, and though the eclectic style wasn't quite to my taste it had a sort of charm to it. *Restore, not remodel.* It was a mindset I'd never had. I was more of the "tear it down and build something new" school of thought—higher, larger, cutting-edge. Nothing of my past had been worth preserving.

"I'll take good care of it."

"May I?" I motioned to the necklace to fasten it for her. Ivy scrutinized me—I'd forgotten how unique the color of her eyes was. I had green/hazel eyes, depending on who you asked, but Ivy's eyes were a stormy gray.

"Sure, I guess," she said. "Just as long as you behave yourself."

"I would never bite you without your express permission," I promised.

"Right." She tensed as I moved behind her and draped the necklace around her scarred throat. I swallowed my anger at the sight of her wounds—I was half tempted to raise the bastard just so I could torture him myself. Raising a vampire was unheard of in necromancer circles, but I had an unusual set of skills.

"You're the one who insists I'm in rehab." I fastened the clasp and stepped away. "I'm atoning for my sins, not adding to the list."

Ivy spun, slinging her legs over the piano bench as faced me. She folded her arms and quirked an eyebrow. "You're admitting to being a vampire bastard?"

"Well, I..." I spotted an overstuffed armchair nearby and retreated to it. "Yes, I suppose I am. There were unique circumstances, but they don't change the things I've done."

She barked a bitter laugh. "Yeah, right. I understand that, more than you know. Our publicists will lose their collective shit at the chance to plan our redemption tours."

I glanced past her at the piano keys. "Are you planning to perform again?"

"Probably not in public." She shrugged. "I left these scars alone but let a witch heal the meaty bits on the inside just enough to allow me to sing again. I can handle recording an album, but performing might be too much strain."

"It changed the sound of your voice."

"It did. Not bad, just different."

My lips quirked. "That should be the theme of our redemption tour—not bad, just different."

She chuckled, a rueful tilt to her smile. "Deal. I'll get the merch made." She sighed and rubbed her palms on her jeans. "I don't...I've spent so long playing the rockstar role. I'm not sure how to be anyone else in public, but it's not *me* anymore. I've changed too much to go back."

"It's hard to rebuild." I nodded in sympathy. At the moment I was too focused on stopping the demon invasion to ponder how my life would change if we were successful. I couldn't go back to the person I was when I was under the influence of Laura's spell. I'd given everything to build a life that I hadn't wanted before I met Laura. What sort of life did I want now? How would Ivy factor into it?

She straightened. "Now that our ghosts are handled, what's the next step?"

I glanced through the nearest window. Overnight the thundersnow had transformed into a blizzard, and a constant blur of white whipped past as the house groaned under the assault of the strong winds.

"Well, any non-magical means of travel will have to wait until the storm subsides. Our magical means are also somewhat limited." I grimaced. Under normal circumstances I could simply shadowstep and evacuate Ivy and her entourage of ghosts and dogs, but the inhabitants of the shadow realm were working with the forces leading the attack on our world. Any travel through the realm was best done in numbers, or with appropriate backup, like Faust and Patience.

"Right, I guess you can't take a shortcut through Faerie."

My brow rose as I tensed. "You're faerie blooded?"

"Possibly a small fraction, but I don't know any details. Paz is faerie blooded. He used to cast portals so we could escape from our hotel rooms when our manager grounded us."

I thanked the higher powers—I didn't need Catherine and her irritating Oberon husband lecturing me about proper care of my soul mate if Ivy had been faerie blooded and fallen under their jurisdiction. I'd already had enough of that from Faust, Patience, Anne, and my least favorite cousin, Simon St. Jerome.

"If the storm clears up, I'll call for my helicopter. If not, we'll have to wait until my faerie uncle and his bride return from their banishing shift tomorrow morning."

"There's a lot to unpack in that statement." Ivy rose and

motioned for me to join her. "You can explain all the things to me while I close up the house and pack for the apocalypse."

"The apocalypse probably won't happen."

"I find your lack of faith disturbing." I frowned, and she rolled her eyes. "What, they didn't allow pop culture in your super-exclusive trust-fund-baby boarding school?"

"Pop culture was considered contraband," I said dryly.

"Shouldn't you have been all about that? Sneaking out of your dorms to smoke weed and discuss heavy metal or something?" She paused to close the curtains in the music room and cover the piano keys with the fallboard. "You strike me as the rebellious youth type. Bad behavior as a cry for your parents' attention."

"Yes and no."

She gathered up the sheet music and stuck it between the pages of a notebook. "Moderately rebellious? Snuck out but didn't inhale?"

I chuckled with a wry smile. "I was an alchemist. I inhaled. And you?"

"High school dropout." She led me from the room and I followed to her bedroom, where she produced a beaten-up, military style duffle bag from her wardrobe. "I did get my GED, though. Eventually."

I searched for a place to sit and settled for a relatively clear spot on the bench at the foot of her bed. Her room was on the edge of being a disaster area—messy, but not filthy. An assortment of black T-shirts, hooded sweatshirts, and jeans were strewn about and collected in piles, but there was no food or dirty dishes. A college friend had been infamous for creating "furniture" from empty pizza boxes in his dorm room—the mice appreciated his art, but his roommate certainly didn't.

"Why did you drop out?" I asked.

"Didn't see a point in staying. Music was all I wanted to do, and there was no way I was going to get into college with my grades."

"Rebellious youth?"

Ivy grinned. "Yes and no. Mom was a single parent and an addict. I had to be the grownup in our relationship when I was little if I wanted to eat or have clean clothes. I was sick of it by the time I was a teenager. All I wanted was out. Freedom."

"And you found it?"

"After a fashion." She stood in front of the open wardrobe, her back to me as she sorted through her T-shirt collection. It rather reminded me of Catherine, who had reacquainted me with blue jeans, because "denim is the American way."

Ivy's two dogs galloped into the room and dove onto the bed. After a moment they seemed to realize that I was present and ambled over to shower me with slobber. I supposed that it was an improvement over the Duquesnes' dogs, who wanted to maul me on sight.

"Hey! Off the bed! You're making a mess." Ivy pointed at the floor, and the dogs obeyed after a moment of canine reluctance. "You are the worst guard dogs ever. You're supposed to bite vampires, not kiss them."

I smirked as the unrepentant pair wagged their tails at their mistress. "I do have that effect on women."

"Ha ha, very funny." She scowled at me and then pointed to a pair of enormous dog beds, both covered with bright pink blankets festooned with images of paw prints, dog bones, and tiaras for some unknown reason. "Go lay down."

"Are they meant to be guard dogs?" I asked.

"In theory. I mean, they're not trained for that, but the paps see them coming and they run the other way."

"Why? They seem perfectly friendly."

"Misconceptions about the breed. Or breeds in their case, considering they're a little bit of everything, including dachshund for some ungodly reason I don't want to picture." Ivy paused and studied me with an anxious expression. "What do you want? About this soul mate thing? What are your expectations?"

I rocked back and ran a hand through my hair, unprepared for the change in topic. "To be honest, I haven't thought past protecting you from the hunters. There's little point in planning for the future if we fail to stop the demons."

"Morbid but accurate, I like it." She placed her hands on her hips as she chewed her bottom lip with a faraway expression. "I'm not ready for planning the future. I'm...well, in the spirit of being honest, I'm still more than a little fucked up about the attack."

"You loved him. The guardian."

"I thought I did." She sighed and flopped to the floor to sit with her legs folded. One of her dogs—Natasha, the one with black fur—padded over and laid in her lap, to Ivy's exasperation and my amusement. To my knowledge, lap dogs were supposed to weigh twenty pounds or less, and Ivy's dogs certainly didn't.

She scratched the dog behind its ears. "Maybe I did? I don't really have a solid point of reference for being in love. I do hookups, not relationships, as you're aware."

I nodded and fought down a wave of bitterness. Ivy had wanted more from me, but I'd avoided her like a coward and ended up under Laura's thumb. I didn't have a point of reference for love, either. I'd thought I loved Catherine, but with the spell broken I now knew that my feelings for Catherine were unhealthy, and my actions unforgivable. It might be impossible to properly apologize for my behavior—Catherine wouldn't believe my sincerity, and her guardian husband would sooner gut me than allow me to make amends.

"I cared about Nick," she said. "I know he cared about me, and it got him killed."

"That's not your fault."

"My stalker, my fault."

"The stalker's fault. You're victim-blaming yourself."

"Ooh, 'victim-blaming', you *are* in rehab."

"Therapy," I corrected. "Though I need to make more time for it."

"Right. Probably hard to see a shrink when the world's ending." She tilted her head. "Am I expected to fight? I'm not bad at self-defense, but an all-out battle with the forces of evil is a tad bit outside my skill set."

"You're a sorceress, if I remember correctly. We can work with that. What element is your specialty?"

She dropped her gaze and concentrated on petting the dog in her lap. Silence stretched, and I wondered if I should repeat the question. "Ice."

Air and water—not well respected in sorcerer society, as they seemed to be obsessed with fire. Any combination of elements could be useful in a fight, and ice particularly so in our battle against demons. As the saying went, one couldn't fight fire with fire.

"I don't do well at letting people in," she said. "I've worn a lot of masks, and not just on stage. I had to be the parent in my relationship since I was old enough to lie to my teacher about why my mom couldn't make it to...well, just about everything. She was always too strung out to attend meetings or plays or whatnot."

Ivy shrugged as though unaffected, but I was all too familiar with that blasé front.

"My uncle attended mine. My parents couldn't be bothered, but Faust always made the effort." I smiled weakly, a slight twitch of my lips—I'd never properly thanked him for that. I hadn't realized the impact he'd had on me, but now, looking back, I knew that he was the single constant in my life.

And I'd tried to kill his soul mate.

I groaned and held my face in my hands. "I suppose I'm guilty of not letting people in and pushing away those few that I have." I breathed deep and straightened to meet Ivy's gaze. "Soul mates aren't guaranteed happiness—they still need to put effort into their relationship to make it successful, just like anyone else. I would like this to work between us if you're willing to try. It won't be simple or easy, but I think it will be worth the effort."

"All right. I can do that." Ivy patted Natasha and nudged the dog off her lap. "Where are we evacuating to?"

"My home outside of Chicago."

"McMansion?"

My brow furrowed as I tried to place the saying—Patience had said something similar in passing once or twice. "Well, it *is* in Oak Brook, where McDonalds' headquarters was located."

Ivy laughed. "Not quite what I meant, but okay. You don't have resident ghosts who'll fight with my ghosts?"

"Ghosts, no. I do have...an assortment of unusual guests seeking sanctuary in my guest house."

"Oh?"

"The hunters have been abducting any magician they can get their hands on. They attempted to capture the new Titania and Oberon, who I am acquainted with." I cleared my throat. "They've been staying in my guest house since, with their assortment of pets and the occasional visit from Catherine's faerie cousin who would very much enjoy killing me."

It was more or less true. They moved in after the attack, stayed for a bit, moved out to stay with Michael and Emily Black until their home was attacked, and now I was hosting all of them in the guest house. The end of the world made for odd bedfellows—or housemates as the case was. Estate-mates?

"That sounds like a dark sitcom. Are they going to have a problem with me?"

"I can't imagine why. For the most part they tolerate my presence now." If nothing else, Mrs. Black had managed to restrain herself from hitting me in the head with a brick again, and Portia Silverleaf was holding herself to one death threat per visit.

"I suggest we take things slowly as far as romance goes," I said. "Neither of us is in a good place to start a new relationship at the moment."

"Or rekindle an old one." Ivy nodded. "Maybe we should sign up for couples counseling now."

I stroked my chin. "It's not a bad idea, though we might not have much time to devote to it."

"Right." Ivy's lips pressed in a thin line and her gaze unfocused as she pondered something for a long moment. Finally she sighed and shook her head. "You're giving me head and heart drama."

"Pardon?"

"I should have kicked your ass off my island on sight," she said. "That would've been the smart thing to do. My head tells me that I have no logical reason to trust you. You're dangerous. You literally belong to the same undead club as the stalker who tried to kill me."

"But?" I asked. I hoped there was a 'but' to that statement because it didn't bode well for our future together.

"But my heart tells me that you're right about the soul

mate thing. It's a jumbled-up mess of feels. Like I know you won't hurt me, despite any supporting evidence. I know I can trust you. It makes me suspicious and prickly and I don't like it."

"I understand. I intend to do everything in my power to prove that you can trust me—and trust us."

"Then I guess we're giving this a shot." Ivy wiped her palms on her jeans. "But for now, I'll pack and you tell me everything I need to know about the end of the world."

"Deal."

CHAPTER FOUR

Ivy

"This isn't about fun," Nick said. "It's about saving your life."

I rolled my eyes at the guardian, and he scowled down at me as though I was a toddler who'd been put in timeout. What good was life without fun? And hot damn, did he ever look like fun—a real Italian stallion. Too bad he had a stick up his ass. I'd met a few guardians in passing before and never realized that they were the fun police in addition to being magic ones. Ugh.

I folded my arms. "We don't know that my life is in danger."

"I wouldn't be here if it wasn't." Nick pulled out a chair and sat backward in it, like a youth pastor trying to relate to the troubled kids doing community service. "We're going to set down a few ground rules—"

"I don't do well with rules."

"Do you do well with dying?"

"Wouldn't know, never tried it."

"Right." Nick sighed and pinched the bridge of his nose. "No drinking. No drugs. No sex. I need to know where you are at all times—"

"What the fuck?" I protested. There was no way I was going to agree to any of that.

"Ivy. You are under my protection. If you don't follow these rules, you could get both of us killed."

I snorted. Yeah, right. Nothing could kill a guardian, they had the higher powers on their side. This whole stalker thing was being blown way out of proportion.

"Yeah, yeah. I get it. Fine." I'd had stalkers before—so what if this one was a vampire?

What was the worst that could happen?

I jolted awake with a gasp and reached for my throat—yup, scars were still there. I stared up at my bedroom ceiling and watched the slowly circling stars of the girls' nightlight.

Damn it all. All signs pointed to me having learned nothing from my time with Nick. His blood was on my hands thanks to my inability to take anything seriously, and what did I do when the next fang-face entered my life?

I kissed him.

In my defense, it seemed the appropriate thing to do at the time. I'd been lulled into a sense of security after the day went reasonably well with only two panic attacks as I prepared to leave the mansion. My bags were packed, the dogs' bags were packed (much to Zach's bemusement), and even the ghosts were ready to go. We enjoyed a quiet dinner, watched a rom com (also much to Zach's bemusement), and at the end of the evening I walked him to the guest room like I was walking a date to their door.

Zach smiled politely. "Thank you for the pleasant evening."

"You're welcome."

The reply was a reflex, but it felt wrong somehow—I was a rock star, I didn't do polite, pleasant evenings. I may have been out of the game since the attack, but I had a reputation to uphold. The awkward moment stretched between us, so I did what felt like the normal thing to do when bidding someone goodnight—I leaned in and kissed him.

All things considered, the kiss was extremely tame compared to the content of our debauched weekend in Vegas—and it didn't help that the more time I spent with him, the more details I remembered of our time together. Obviously, the sexual gymnastics had been memorable, but there were smaller, more intimate details, like the way the corners of his eyes crinkled when he was amused. Lord and Lady, those eyes—vibrant, summer green with warm brown flecks. He looked so damn alive that it was almost easy to forget that he wasn't.

The kiss was soft and sweet and hesitant, until it wasn't. As a rule I didn't do sweet—I was rough and eager, always ready for more—so the kiss deepened and I moaned into Zach's mouth as I chased the taste of him. *This*—the mysterious something extra that I'd noticed during our weekend together but hadn't been able to identify had to be our soul mate connection. The spark that had ignited between us six years ago rekindled as heat spread through my limbs and pooled in my core.

I wanted more, but some shriveled, forgotten sense of self-preservation reared its head and reminded me that even a tempting vampire was still a damn vampire, and I needed to keep my hands to myself.

"Whoops." I stepped back and cleared my throat. "Sorry. Got a little carried away."

"No apology necessary." Zach blushed—how the hell did a vampire blush? "Good night, Ivy. Sleep well."

We parted ways and I returned to my room. I tossed and turned until I finally dozed off, comforted by the knowledge that we were being evacuated to safety when his faerie relatives arrived in the morning—and wasn't that bizarre? Faerie relatives. I'd met a few faeries over the years, because apparently I had a few faerie fans, who knew? But faerie relatives? My brain struggled to wrap around that idea.

I rolled over and stared at the clock on my nightstand—3:33 AM. Great. I flopped back with a sigh and then nearly had a heart attack as my fur babies went from sound asleep to losing their absolute shit in the blink of an eye. They leaped from their dog beds, full-on "I'm gonna maul that guy" barking as they charged the bedroom door.

My first thought was intruders—during the summer we'd had two enterprising paparazzi who managed to worm their way past my security, right up to the house, but were promptly chased off by Natasha and Yelena. I grabbed the pistol from my nightstand and tried to flip on the lights just as the room went completely black. The power was out again, and this time it wasn't my fault.

The girls snarled at the door as though they intended to tear apart the danger on the other side, and I opened it and let them rocket into the dark hallway. I held my gun like Nick had taught me—two hands for stability, finger off the trigger until I had a target I intended to shoot—and scanned the hallway. Completely black. Not helpful.

I eased along the wall, intending to find Zach, when he yelled, "Get down!"

I dropped like a good soldier—again, like Nick had taught me—and I broke out in a cold sweat at the similarities between this attack and the one he'd died in. *Fuck, I couldn't do this again...*

A fireball whooshed overhead and my intended warning to not burn my damn house down died in my throat when I saw the spell splash against a creature of pure darkness. My heart kicked into overdrive and my pulse thudded in my ears. What was worse than a vampire invasion? Evil minions from a hell dimension, that's what.

I gaped at the shrieking demon and then unleashed a scream of my own when someone grabbed my arm. Zach hauled me to my feet. "This way."

"There's more?" I blurted.

"There are always more."

Thunder rumbled as if confirming his words, and I'd already had enough of this bullshit. My teeth ground as I followed Zach toward the sound of my snarling babies.

I stumbled and cursed. "Some of us can't see in the dark, Vlad."

He huffed a put-upon sigh and I half expected him to bust out a line from *Dracula* in reply. We reached the landing of the grand staircase and looked down. My skin tingled where Zach gripped my arm, and suddenly I had magic night vision. I blinked, and as the scene came into focus. A squad of five armed men in black tactical gear and goggles stood in formation in the foyer, like one of Paz's military shooter video games come to life. Great. I was a mission objective.

Scowling, I dropped to one knee, braced against the stair rail, and aimed for one of the home invaders. Nick's instructions whispered through my mind as I took my shot. I missed my target and hit body armor instead of a weak spot, and the hunters (had to be the hunters) turned toward me. Zach zipped down the stairs in a blur and tore into the nearest one. I fired a few more times, and a freaking tranq dart thudded into the hand-carved oak baluster beside my face.

"Assholes! That's original to the house!"

Enraged, I set the gun down and drew down the power of the storm outside. The hunters weren't going to play nice, so neither was I. Power surged through my body and crackled around me in a whirling shield of ice and snow. So much for sobriety—channeling a storm is the highest high. I felt like a wrathful goddess about to rain devastation upon my enemies.

I encased two hunters in magical ice while Zach and my canine security team downed three others in quick succession, but then all hell broke out—literally. Natasha and Yelena yelped as a trio of oily demons oozed up from the floor like sentient tar and formed humanoid shapes, and the dogs wisely ran for cover. Good—I couldn't fault them for not wanting to tangle with the forces of hell, because they're dogs, not summoners.

Zach rounded on two of the demonic attackers, and I stalked toward the odd demon out as spikes of ice burst from my skin like I'd suddenly become an arctic porcupine.

"Buddy, you picked the wrong house."

The demon grinned, its mouth full of long, white needle teeth worthy of a Guillermo del Toro movie that were shockingly bright in the darkness, and I had a moment of "oh shit" pause.

Sharp teeth tore into my throat as my gaze was glued to the sight of Nick inches away, his body unnaturally still and his neck bent at a sickening angle.

No. Not now. Not ever again. With a furious war cry, I attacked, swinging, dodging, and cursing. I think I startled him—guess the demon hadn't figured I'd be a hostile target, that Zach would be the fighter and I'd cower like some spoiled damsel. After the demon recovered from its surprise, it launched its counterattack. It landed a solid strike to my jaw, and my mouth filled with blood and I swore I saw cartoon birds circle my head. I spat the blood at the demon and grappled him in a bear hug, and my ice spikes pierced his greasy shadow skin.

"Get out of my house and go back to hell."

The demon howled and melted like a wicked witch with a

water allergy. I slapped at my clothes because eww, the bastard left behind greasy demon stains as he oozed away. My freakout was interrupted as Zach cried out in pain, and I whirled toward him. He doubled over, clutching his torso as though attempting to hold his guts in, and then he fell to his knees.

Nick and the vampire moved like a hurricane, their attacks too fast to track. The vamp was powerful—old enough to have gained enough wealth and influence to cover his crimes, the murdering fuck—and moved in a blur of fangs and claws. Nick's guardian strength and speed met the vamp blow for blow, until the fight ended with a sickening wet crack.

Nick collapsed, and I was alone.

Zach slumped to the floor and my mind went white as my brittle control snapped. I became the storm—howling wind, blinding snow, ice and frozen fury. Power poured through my veins and I threw raw magic at the remaining demons. They staggered under the onslaught and one disintegrated into ooze. The last demon standing closed the distance between us and landed a punch to my torso that I knew I'd feel later, but I was too far gone to care. I grabbed his face and my icy talons sank into sticky shadow flesh and bone.

"Tell them." The words crackled through the air between us like breaking ice. The demon's eyes widened as the frost from my breath covered the oily skin of his face like a spreading plague. "My words are poison."

The frost raced across the demon's skin until he was encased in ice, and then I squeezed and the monster broke apart like a macabre puzzle. I stepped back and laughed, drunk on power as it raged through my body.

"Control it." The memory of my mother's voice whispered through the howling wind. *"You have to control it, or it'll consume you."*

Like it consumed her and every other tempest who'd ever lived—chewed her up, spit her out and left her a broken shell forever chasing the next high. Right. I threw my head back and screamed as I struggled to pull myself back and disconnect. Sensing my distress, Natasha and Yelena bounded toward me and collided with my legs, and I reached out and stroked their short, soft fur to ground myself.

"Good girls," I murmured.

I shook off the last of the magic and wobbled toward Zach. I kneeled at his side and he groaned and coughed, and dark blood speckled his mouth like spilled ink. Stab wounds covered his torso from his neck to his waist, and my hands hovered over him, unsure of which wound to put pressure on first. He rasped something unintelligible and fell still. I hissed in fear and frustration as panic squeezed my chest. Damn it, we just started working on this soul mate thing, he wasn't allowed to die on me. My dogs whined—sadly, they didn't know any vampire first aid, either.

For a moment—one single, awful moment—the thought that I could let him die flashed through my mind. If Zach died, I wouldn't have to cope with having a vampire soul mate. I shoved the thought away with a snarl, because yeah I was a bitch, but I wasn't a fucking evil bitch.

Help, we needed help. "Faust!" I called for Zach's faerie uncle, held my breath and then exhaled a frustrated sigh. I tried a few more times to no effect, added his aunt-in-law's name, and still nothing. Maybe you had to be faerie blooded to call a faerie? The storm raged outside so I knew cell service was still fucked. I tried one last call for help, a last-ditch attempt with a different name.

"Helen?" I shouted. "Hey! Helen Harrison! Your son needs you. Get your faerie ass in gear!"

A curvaceous blonde popped out of nowhere, as though

I'd accidentally summoned the spirt of Marilyn Monroe. My jaw dropped—first, because holy shit that worked, and two, because Helen looked like a bizarre combination of an ancient Greek goddess and the Real Housewives of Troy. "Oh, my sweet boy! What happened?"

"Demons. Fix him."

Her perfect nose wrinkled. "I've never had any skill at healing. That Titania he's so fond of should suffice."

Before I could voice the warning that Zach said not to go through the shadow realm without a group, the faerie snapped her fingers, and we were all instantly transported into a spacious sitting room with modern monochrome décor down to the tasteful throw pillows in varying shades of gray. The electricity here was working, good, but Zach and I instantly made of mess of the white shag carpet. White carpet? For fuck's sake—

"I always did despise that wallpaper." Helen frowned at the room. "It's so pedestrian."

"Fuck the wallpaper! Save your son."

She waved a dismissive hand. "He'll be fine after proper medical attention. He's been in worse scraps than this."

A pair of dogs—not mine—bounded into the room and appeared confused by our presence. Natasha and Yelena were still too on-edge to make friends. A couple in rumpled sleeping attire, the woman sporting a baby bump, followed the new arrivals.

"Ah, there they are," Helen said. "Titania, my son requires healing."

"Your—what?" The Titania in question blinked blearily at the scene.

"Fix him," I said. "He's dying."

The couple turned their attention to me, and to Zach's unconscious form next to me. The Oberon, presumably, folded his arms. "He's a vampire," he drawled. "He's already dead."

And for the second time in less than ten minutes, I lost my shit. I hissed like an angry cat and power exploded from my hands and arced to the surrounding electric fixtures. Light bulbs exploded, electricity crackled, and the power surged.

"Fix him. *Now.*"

"All right, keep your shirt on." The Titania smacked her husband's arm. "Call Amelia, tell her to get her team together." She crossed to us and slowly kneeled, probably off-balanced by her baby bump. She started some sort of witch magic that I didn't recognize—Paz might be a witch, but aside from curing hangovers and easing muscle cramps, there's not a lot of healing going on when we're on tour.

"You must be my Zachary's soul mate," Helen said.

I glanced up, expecting her to be as focused on his recovery as I was, but instead the faerie eyed me with the expression of a predator who'd found interesting prey. I swallowed hard. Faeries were old enough to recognize my powers for what they were. I wasn't a true sorceress—tempests were like a subspecies of sorcerer—and my kind were supposed to be extinct.

"Here now, you look a dreadful mess," Helen said. "The Titania has this well in hand. Why don't we retire to Zachary's chambers and get you cleaned up?"

"Wait," the Titania said, but not fast enough. Helen snapped us into what was presumably Zach's bedroom, including my dogs, which I was still vaguely surprised by, and my ghosts, because I was wearing Jordan's necklace. The poor ghosts definitely looked shellshocked by the demons and teleporting and other magical shenanigans.

Helen tsked and shook her head at the black and white

décor—clean lines, zero personality. "Honestly, Zachary. One would think you were colorblind."

I rose and caught my reflection in the mirror above Zach's black lacquered dresser, and I gasped. I hundred percent looked like the final girl in a horror flick. Was I hurt? Did I care?

"You do look a fright, poor child. Come with me."

I followed her into the master bath, and I nodded in silent approval of the layout—I was always a fan of a palatial bathroom. I made a beeline for the marble sink and washed the blood from my hands.

"What is your name, my dear?"

I half-remembered something about never telling a faerie your true name, but I had that covered because my stage name wasn't my birth name. "Ivy Taylor."

"And does Zachary know what you are?"

I flinched and splashed water on my equally bloody face. "A lead singer?"

Helen laughed, and the sound was half musical, half menacing. "Oh, yes of course, your musical group. You're quite popular, from what I understand. A good match for my darling boy. I would have hated to see him matched with some peasant incapable of existing amongst the wealthy and powerful."

I swallowed the urge to cuss her out, since I was in fact a peasant, but I was aware enough not to taunt the clearly unstable faerie.

"Have you met the rest of our little family?"

"Not yet." I grabbed a washcloth, soaped it up and concentrated on scrubbing the stubborn spots clean. "Zach and I just reconnected."

"You two had met before?"

"Yes. Right before his mentor sank her undead claws in him."

Helen snarled, and the dogs whined and retreated into the bedroom. Yeah—if my dogs didn't like someone, there was always a good reason.

"That gold-digging whore. I despised her." Helen clenched her delicate hands into fists and I swore the room trembled as though experiencing low-grade earthquake. "She was unworthy of my dear boy. I should have killed her when I had the opportunity."

I swallowed hard. *Note to self, do not anger future mother-in-law.* I cleared my throat. "Yeah, she sounded like a real bitch. She even cast some kind of mind-control spell over him."

Helen growled. "Well, that would explain why he sent me away. It must have been her command." She straightened and smiled sweetly, mood changing with the flip of a switch. "Not that it matters now. I'm here, and together you and I will ensure his safety. Though it does beg the question of where my brother is. He was supposed to be keeping watch over Zachary. Faust!"

Please, no. Not another crazy faerie.

"He didn't answer me earlier," I said.

She scowled and called for Faust again, and a pair of faeries tumbled into the master bathroom, along with two magicians, none of whom I recognized.

"Sister?" the faerie I assumed was Faust asked. The round, mirrored lenses of his glasses were cracked and the ends of his spiked black hair were singed and smoking. "What's wrong?"

"You were supposed to be watching him," Helen snapped.

The red-headed faerie with giant flaming butterfly wings, mostly likely Faust's soul mate, Patience, whistled low. "Hoo boy. Okay, kids, let's back away slowly and let them rumble without us."

Patience apparently included me among the kids and motioned for me to get while the getting was good, and I decided that discretion was the better part of valor and high-tailed it to the bedroom.

"Your concern for my wellbeing is touching," Faust said dryly to his spouse, who shrugged.

"I'm pregnant, I'm bowing out of this one." Having successfully shooed the mortals out, she stuck her head into the bathroom before closing the door. "Okay, I love you, bye now!"

I turned and got a better look at Patience and Faust's companions, a young Latina wearing army surplus attire accompanied by a frowning hot guy dressed in all black.

"Are these your dogs?" The young woman bent to pet Natasha and Yelena, who wriggled with doggie bliss under her attention.

"Yeah," I said. "We were being attacked by hunters and demons, and now we're here, and to be honest, this is all a bit much."

"Don't doubt it. I'm Nati, and this is my boyfriend Cris." She motioned to the man beside her, who nodded politely despite continuing to eye me with disapproval.

"Where's bizarro Bruce Wayne?" Patience asked.

I blinked and assumed she meant Zach. "With a healer. He was really torn up."

The faerie tilted her head and studied me from behind a pair of wirerimmed sunglasses while her companions shuffled uneasily. "A demon got the drop on Harrison?"

"Three demons. They were really big?" I shrugged, though I had no previous demon experience as a point of reference.

"Damn it. That can't be good." Patience pinched the bridge of her nose and sighed. "I'm hungry. Let's go raid the kitchen while we all get better acquainted."

CHAPTER FIVE

Zach

I groaned when I clawed my way back to consciousness. I scrubbed my gummy eyes, and then flinched as the person hovering over me came into focus.

"Mother? What are you doing here?"

"Oh, my sweet boy." She patted my hand and I swallowed the urge to tell her to drop the act. I was well aware that Fair Helen had the maternal instincts of a shark. "Your uncle was delinquent in watching over you, and your clever soul mate called for my aid. She's a lovely girl." She smiled, and my stomach sank. Helen had never approved of any of my girlfriends, up to and including Laura. I had no idea how to process this development.

"Where's Ivy?"

"She's resting in your rooms. She was injured, and I imagine it was quite the fright for her, poor dear."

I flinched and tried to sit up. "Injured how?"

"Calm yourself, Zachary." Helen nudged my shoulder until I settled. "Ivy suffered a few scrapes and bruises, nothing serious."

I peered at the room. I was back at my home in Oak Brook, in one of the estate's healing rooms. I needed blood, which meant I needed my apprentice. I weighed the immediacy of my hunger against exposing Anthony to Helen. Then again, the boy did need practice in dealing with monsters. Grimacing, I called for Anthony through our bond and waited.

Helen peered at me, one slender, well-manicured finger tapping at her chin—nothing good would come from that expression.

"Yes, Mother?"

"You did remember to preserve some of your—oh, what did he call it? Ah, yes, 'genetic legacy' before you became this, didn't you?"

Mortified, I fought the urge to pull the pillow over my face and hide, just like I'd done as a child when my parents were arguing. The "he" in this equation must have been Faust. I knew he kept my mother informed about my welfare, but discussing my deposit in the sperm bank was a bridge too far. In that moment I wished for a quick death, but unfortunately I was already dead.

"Yes, Mother," I said flatly. "I thought you were opposed to being a grandmother."

"Oh, but your children with Ivy will be marvelous! And it's so much simpler being a grandmother. All the joys of motherhood with none of the parenting work."

"You didn't do any of the parenting before." I glared at her, but she waved my comment away.

"Shush now, darling. Save that energy for healing. I expect we have quite the battle approaching."

We? Oh no...

Anthony arrived and paused in the doorway. "Master?"

The corners of my mouth twitched—Anthony was a good

student, and a trusted friend. We weren't formal in private, but he had been trained to switch to proper address when in the presence of unfamiliar magicians.

"Is this your student?" Helen brightened and favored Anthony with her radiant, empty smile. "Come here, young one, let me see you."

Help, please, he squeaked over the bond.

Can't, I replied. *There's no avoiding her. Helen is inevitable.*

As if on cue, she patted Anthony's cheek and then motioned for him to turn around to be inspected like a slave at auction. Faust was tight-lipped on the subject of Helen's previous history, but I could easily imagine her as a plantation owner. She had a love of wealth and fine things, and zero appreciation for human life.

"Do I pass muster, Mrs. Harrison?" Anthony asked.

She waved the question away. "Oh, do call me Helen. I divorced Zachary's father ages ago. Now, you do seem like a fine young man. Are you certain you wish to pursue necromancy? It's so distasteful."

"Mother—"

She frowned at me. "I'm still cross with you, though I suppose it may have saved your life this time. That does not excuse the many other times that your chosen path has endangered it."

"My choice, not yours. Now, I need to speak with Anthony. Perhaps you can check in with Faust and he can update you on our plans for dealing with the demons."

"Hmm. I suppose. Though that woman he married is so grating." Helen shuddered for dramatic effect, and Anthony snorted, likely in agreement. Patience Roberts was difficult to interact with under the best circumstances, and that was before I'd tried to kill her.

"Please," I added.

"Oh, very well." Helen brushed a kiss on my forehead and then vanished. I tried to remember the last time she'd shown that sort of affection toward me and couldn't come up with an example.

"How're you feeling, boss?" Anthony asked.

"Like I've been pummeled by an ancient demon."

"Two demons, from what I heard. They weren't really ancient demons, were they?"

"No, thank the powers." I grunted as I eased myself into sitting up and slowly swung my legs over the side of the bed. "I think we're still lucky enough that only one ancient demon has gotten through thus far. These were powerful, though. Did Ivy say how she banished them?"

It seemed unlikely—by all reports, Ivy's strength and skill as a sorceress were average, and that couldn't have been enough to banish the demons we faced. Maybe she'd called Helen in to finish the job after I collapsed?

"No. Everyone's in the guest house freaking out, and she hasn't been back there since you two popped in and stained the rug. Patience drew an outline around it like a body in an old-school crime show."

"Of course she did."

"Need a top off?" Anthony smirked and held out his wrist.

"Yes, thank you. I apologize—"

"No apologies necessary. Especially if I can get your soul mate's autograph."

"You've never asked for my autograph." As Catherine liked to harangue me about, I was "famous for being famous." I would define it as famous for being wealthy, attractive and charming.

"No offense, boss, but the lead singer of Poison Apples' autograph scores far more points at school than yours would."

"Fair enough."

~

I checked on Ivy—fast asleep in my bed, with her two damp canine companions perfuming the air with eau de wet dog. Ivy's ghosts perked up upon my arrival.

"What happened?" Jay asked. "Were those things really demons?"

"Where are we?" Jordan added.

"You're in my estate in Oak Brook, Illinois," I said. "And yes, they were. Did you see what happened?"

Jordan shook her head. "We hid. What were we going to do? Knock aggressively at them? Shout insults?"

Jay shrugged. "All we knew was that one moment we were there and the next we were here, and you were very wounded. You look much improved, by the way, old sport."

"Thanks." I smiled dryly. "I'm going to check in with the others. You're welcome to wander the grounds, but my apprentice is staying here and I haven't informed him of your presence. He's still relatively new to necromancy, but I can't guarantee he won't poke at you."

"So noted," Jay said. "Safe travels."

One of the dogs—Natasha—perked up and decided to accompany me on my trip to the guest house. I didn't argue, because Catherine and her Silverleaf cousin, Portia, were both animal lovers, and Natasha's presence might buy me some good will.

Alexander Duquesne, on the other hand, was going to despise me until his last breath.

I let myself in and followed the sound of raised voices to the sitting room and discovered that Anthony was correct—a pink glitter outline formed a body around the blood stain where I must have lain, complete with cartoon fangs and two x's for eyes. With a sigh I paused in the doorway, and Natasha sat beside me. I wasn't an animal lover, but I did appreciate how well-trained Ivy's dogs were. I can't imagine that many dogs would willingly attack a demon. Aside from the Duquesnes' dogs, who were studying Natasha with tilted heads.

"What are we arguing about?" I asked.

"You!" Portia Silverleaf began but was instantly distracted. "You have a puppy! When did you get a puppy?"

"Natasha belongs to Ivy." I watched, bemused, as the faerie flittered over and conjured a squeaky toy—a plush vampire—and offered it to Natasha. This was going to be a very long day.

Duquesne folded his arms and glared at me. "What happened?"

"I'm feeling much better, Alexander. Thank you for asking."

Catherine placed a hand on her husband's arm before he could snarl a reply. "Yes, yes, we're all very happy that you continue to be only mostly dead, but we do need to know what happened. And how your mom got involved. She's..."

"Awful?" I suggested. "A magician Stepford wife? A WASP on faerie steroids?"

"Aww, see, you do know pop culture!" Catherine grinned.

And at that moment my other tenants, Mr. and Mrs. Black, arrived, and I realized just how dangerous my mother's presence had the potential to be. War made for strange allies, and under normal circumstances Michael and Emily Black would be considered my enemies due to their particular history with my faerie family. Helen was likely to attack them on sight.

I cursed. "Does she know they're here?" I asked Catherine.

"What seems to be the matter now?" Michael asked.

"My mother is here," I said.

"And that's...bad?" Emily guessed.

"She's Faust's sister," I said. "Helen."

Their eyes widened while the Duquesnes frowned in confusion.

I sighed. "Mrs. Black's testimony against my mother got her clan declared spadowspawn and banished from Faerie."

"I beg your pardon," Emily said. "I do believe it was Helen's actions that were at fault."

Catherine held her hands up. "Whoa, time out. The apocalypse is still approaching. We don't have time for drama over who did what to who a hundred years ago."

"Over one hundred, actually," Michael added.

"Doesn't matter." Catherine turned to me. "Is she going to be a problem?"

I nodded. "She's always a problem."

"Guess the apple didn't fall far from the tree," Duquesne drawled.

Old anger singed my skin as my fists clenched, and I inhaled a shaky, centering breath. He had a right to be angry. I was at fault.

I folded my hands. "Fortunately, Helen seems enamored of Ivy at the moment, so that might prove to be a strong enough distraction to avoid bloodshed." *For now*, I added silently.

Emily frowned. "I do believe your soul mate has been through enough without adding Helen to her burden."

"Agreed, but there is little we can do at the moment," I said. "We're running out of time. The demons controlling the hunters in this attack were far stronger than the ones we've recently encountered. Perhaps a few centuries shy from becoming ancient demons."

Catherine spouted a string of curses, and her husband

wrapped an arm around her shoulders and pulled her into an embrace.

"How did you banish them?" Michael asked.

"I didn't. I assume Helen did when she arrived."

Duquesne turned to Portia. "Could you banish an almost-ancient demon?"

"Don't know." She shrugged, the motion shedding ice faerie dust over the already damaged carpet. She was seated on the floor, surrounded by the dogs as she played tug-of-war with them. "Never tried it before."

"Has there been any update from the faerie Council of Three?"

"Nope!" Portia conjured another toy and offered it to the Duquesnes' German Shepherd.

"They keep blowing us off." Catherine's voice was muffled by her husband's chest.

"This matter is time sensitive," I said.

"I'm aware, Zachary," she snapped in reply. "We're doing everything we can."

"Should we be preparing for the possibility that the faeries will leave us to our fate?" I asked.

Portia scowled and pelted me with a slobber-soaked dog toy. "No! Some of us will fight regardless of their decision."

"*Some* won't be enough to seal off the hell realms."

"We'll get it done," Catherine said. I didn't share her confidence.

"Do you have any other questions?" I asked.

"Not right now. I'd like to talk to your girlfriend when she wakes up."

I quirked a brow. Technically Ivy was my soul mate and not my girlfriend since we weren't officially dating. Two days together trapped by a snowstorm does not a relationship make.

"I'll let her know. If you'll excuse me." I called for Natasha, and to my surprise the dog listened and returned to my side. Did she know I was Ivy's soul mate? Some sort of canine sixth sense? My track record with animals was shaky at best, but Ivy's dogs had taken an immediate liking to me.

Natasha accompanied me back to the main house and my bedroom. She immediately returned to her position on the bed, and I peered at Ivy as she continued to sleep. Someone must have cast a sleeping spell over her because I couldn't imagine her voluntarily sleeping so soundly after our attack. I decided to let soul mates and sleeping dogs lie, and I gathered a change of clothes and headed to the bathroom to clean up.

CHAPTER SIX

Ivy

I woke to the sensation of being surrounded by snoring dogs, but the familiarity ended there. I cracked my eyes open and peered at an unfamiliar ceiling, and then turned my head and spotted Zach in a chair across the room, frowning at a laptop, his socked feet propped up on an ottoman. Very domestic.

"Are you okay?" I asked. My just-woke-up voice was a little on the gravelly side, but it functioned.

"I could ask the same of you." He closed the laptop and set it aside. "How are you feeling?"

"Fine. You were the one who got mauled by evil incarnate."

He huffed a laugh. "True. I'm well enough now. I employ a healing staff for just such an occasion. They've been working overtime lately."

I sat up and scratched Yelena behind her blonde ears—after Staffordshire terrier, her next largest percentage of canine DNA was yellow lab—and her tail thumped on the blanket. "Yeah, I bet. I don't suppose any of my gear made it here?"

"It did, in fact. It's in the guest room across the hall. Faust and Patience picked it up when they cleared your place of evidence of the fight."

Of the bodies. Gross. How many people had died in my haunted mansion now? Was it in the double digits? Was I going to be haunted by the ghostly Gatsbys *and* magician hunters?

I reached up and found that I was still wearing my enchanted necklace. Haunted necklace? Whatever. "Are my ghosts okay?"

"Yes, they're with my apprentice, Anthony. He won't harm them. I think your ghosts are as enamored of him as he is by them. It's not often that spirits willingly interact with a necromancer."

Apprentice. Good, that meant the guy was just a vampire in training and not undead yet.

"If you're feeling well enough, I can have breakfast brought up for you."

"Sure. Breakfast, then a tour?" I glanced down at my canine bedmates. "Do you have dog food? Though really they deserve a steak breakfast. They were very good girls."

Natasha and Yelena burst out in Staffy smiles and decided to shower me with kisses. I allowed it.

"The kitchen borrowed some dog food from the Duquesnes. Let the staff know if you prefer a specific brand. They've also been outside a few times while you slept. Your dogs seem to get along well with our other canine guests. I will admit, it was amusing to watch Natasha assert dominance."

I scratched under her chin. "That's right, you show them who the boss bitch is."

Zach rose. "If you're ready, I'll escort you to your room and you can freshen up."

I frowned—my memory was fuzzy about how I ended up in Zach's bed in the first place. "Why aren't I there now? I don't remember passing out in here."

"Helen cast a sleep spell so you could rest peacefully. I imagine that's her idea of helping." Zach winced. "She seems quite fond of you, which is unprecedented."

"And that's...bad?"

"It's concerning."

Great. Because a crazy faerie mother-in-law was just what this relationship needed. I slowed to a stop and froze in the hallway between our rooms. "Wait...you're actually half faerie. Like, for real. I didn't realize it before, I thought you were omitting the 'x times removed' thing that most faerie-blooded people do. I didn't think that halfblooded was a thing outside of stories."

"Yes, it's rare in modern times. Though it may make a comeback if we manage to survive the apocalypse." He opened the door and the girls galloped through to investigate.

Very nice—it wasn't just a room, but a suite. A small sitting/dining room plus office as the outer room, with the bed and bath presumably beyond. The décor was upscale but impersonal—it could've easily been a hotel suite instead of a room in someone's home. No family photos, no souvenirs, just soothing shades of beige with a few faded pastel highlights.

"This is, what? The lady of the manor's rooms?" I quirked an eyebrow, and I swear he blushed. Now that we weren't surrounded by the distraction of a howling storm keying up my magic and the fear of an impending attack, I was finally calm enough to process small details that my jittery mind skipped over before.

He opened his mouth to answer and I rudely cut him off. "Hold the phone, how can you blush? And why are you awake during the day? And how the fuck were you out in sunlight when you showed up? Granted, it was Michigan winter 'sunlight', but still, it should've at least crisped you like a chicken wing."

Zach sighed. "I'll be happy to answer your questions over breakfast. Did you want to order steak for Natasha and Yelena? Do they have a set meal schedule that the kitchen should be aware of?"

"Just dog food for now, I can work out the steak details with them later, maybe for dinner."

The dogs stayed with Zach while I dressed and tamed my hair into a fashionable (messy) bun. I even slathered on some makeup for the first time in...ouch, that long? There didn't seem a point to it when it was just me and the dogs (and the ghosts) on my tiny island.

Zach dutifully schooled me in Everything You Need to Know about Vampires 101—first lesson, don't call them vampires. They didn't like it because becoming a master necromancer took time and study and the ritual had a very real chance of killing the subject permanently, and the term vampire disrespected their accomplishment. Sort of like calling someone with a PhD a "college graduate."

I scarfed down a feast of scrambled eggs, crispy bacon, and pancakes. When I asked him about the hearty diner-style breakfast, he sighed and claimed it was the Titania's doing.

My brow rose. "What exactly is it between you and the Titania and Oberon? Because he was extra dickish to you when you were bleeding out and that seems like a poor quality in a leader."

Zach grimaced. "He has a right to be. My behavior before the fragmented control spell was removed was...unforgivable."

"Isn't the whole point of a 'not guilty by reason of mental disease' verdict is to not punish you for actions you had no control over?"

"I'm not certain that 'no control' is accurate for my condition." He leaned back in his chair and scrubbed his face with his hands, as though trying to scour away the grime left behind by the spell. "I may have been influenced, but the choices were mine. The actions were mine. Not only did I do horrible things, but I *enjoyed* them."

"Admitting that you have a problem and your life's become unmanageable is the first step."

He huffed a laugh. "I suppose I was addicted to power. Am," he corrected. "I still am."

Yeah, I could relate to that one—I should check the local weather for incoming winter storms. I reached across the table and took his hand. "We're both addicts. I could be your sponsor. I've been down the rehab road before." I smiled dryly. "Quitting is easy, I do it all the time."

Zach squeezed my hand. "Thank you."

Our tender moment was promptly ruined by an invasion of faeries. Faust and Patience were dressed for fashionable murder, and they were accompanied by a frost faerie who had clearly escaped from an '80s Madonna music video.

Zach sighed. "Really?"

The frost faerie squealed, "Doggies!" and my traitorous girls tackled her with kisses.

"Shut up, nephew, you need to see this," Patience replied.

She thrust a tablet into Zach's hands, and his eyes widened. Guess breakfast was over. I tossed my linen napkin next to my plate and circled around the table to peer over Zach's shoulder. The screen displayed footage from a local news traffic copter, but instead of hovering over an expressway the focus was on a snow-covered, well-appointed estate, with a growing mob of people gathering outside the stone fence and wrought-iron gate. My first thought—*oh shit, I hope those people don't have torches and pitchforks*—vanished when I read the ticker scrolling at the bottom of the video.

New Power Couple? Ivy Taylor Out of Hiding, Seen Shacking Up with Zachary Harrison.

"What the actual fuck?" I sputtered. "How is that even possible? I've been here for less than twelve hours!"

"The house isn't bugged, we checked," Patience said.

Faust grimaced. "We suspect it's the hunters. After their attempt to capture Miss Taylor failed, they decided to unleash the media hounds to force you to go to ground where they can closely monitor you."

As if on cue, my phone started ringing in the other room—my PR firm's ringtone.

"Shit!" I hurried three steps in its direction before pausing and spinning on my heel to face Zach. "Call your PR team. We're going to need to release a joint statement saying...something."

"That we're engaged?" Zach suggested with a smirk.

"Too soon. Tabloids will think we're both on a bender and made poor life choices."

"Is that a yes but not now?"

"Ooh, more weddings!" The frost faerie squealed with joy. "I love weddings."

"More?" I asked.

Faust nodded. "There has been an outbreak of weddings, engagements, and pregnancies these past few months."

"Not in that order," Patience said.

"Last-night-on-earth sex?" I guessed.

Patience cackled. "No kidding. My honey knocked me up after we got married in Vegas."

"Elvis chapel?" I asked.

Zach's phone started vibrating in place on the table, and he grimaced. "Joint statement first. Better answer yours as well."

"Right, right. On it."

The rest of the morning flew by in a series of conference calls as my people and Zach's people composed a press release. Then I called my manager (who wasn't a magician) to warn him about the paparazzi explosion, and then each of my bandmates (who were all magicians) to update them about the press and about the oncoming demon apocalypse. As fellow occupants of the hunters' top five most wanted list, the rest of Poison Apples was being offered protection by their local magician authorities. I pondered asking Zach if he could take them in as well, but putting all the high-value eggs in the target basket was probably a terrible idea.

Being a magician in the non-magical limelight was a complex dance. Western magic users had been in hiding since the Burning Times, when the church literally published a book on how to hunt us and hundreds, possibly thousands, of magicians were murdered (along with innocent non-magicians). Magician society was convinced that secrecy equaled safety because we were super outnumbered by the non-magical majority, and as a nearly extinct brand of magician I agreed with that motto—in theory. The band and I hadn't wanted to be dive bar and Renaissance fair famous, we wanted to be rockstars, and now as I frowned at the TV to gauge the progress of the growing mob of fans and reporters, I really missed being small town famous.

I couldn't see the crowd from the window—whoever had designed the layout of Zach's estate had done a good job, and a small forest of trees blocked the view of the road from the house. The local police eventually showed up for crowd control and shooed most of the fans away, but the media persisted. Fuckers.

Someone placed a sandwich in front of me during what had to have been lunchtime, but other than that I was too frazzled to keep track of time. I'd spent a year as a hermit with only dogs and ghosts to talk to, and this was social overload. My hands shook from a combination of adrenaline, anxiety and the desperate need for a drink, a smoke, or any of the vices I used to indulge in.

As if sensing my distress, Zach appeared after my last call, gently plucked the phone from my grasp and then held my hands in his. He was warm—how the hell was he warm? Shouldn't vampires be corpse cold? My stalker certainly was. I shuddered at the memory of icy fingers clamping on to my throat and—

Zach wrapped his arms around me and rubbed my back. "I'm sorry."

"Why, what did you do?" I asked, and he chuckled.

"My sins are legion, but in this case I meant involving you in all of this."

I opened and shut my mouth. *It's okay* wasn't appropriate because none of this was okay. Well, maybe the soul mates thing was okay. The jury was still out on how I felt about that, but with Zach's arms around me in a comforting embrace I was leaning toward soul mates being a potential positive. Maybe.

"It's not your fault," I said. "You didn't put me on the

hunters' kill list. Poison Apples did that all by ourselves." I leaned back and managed a wry smile. "When we were first climbing the charts, we got all kinds of shit from various magician councils about how we were idiots who were endangering all of magiciankind by drawing attention to ourselves."

"I'm familiar with that lecture. I got it first from the alchemists, then from the necromancers."

Of course he did. I sighed and rested my forehead against his chest. "So. What's next?"

"Pan-magician council meeting."

"How are we supposed to manage that with the media wolves at our door?"

"Oh, it's worse than that," Zach said. "The house is now surrounded in the shadow realm. Faust and Patience popped there and immediately returned, with a solid verdict of 'nope' as I recall."

I groaned and winced. Yup, there was the headache that'd been brewing all day.

"What do we do?" I asked. "Conference call?"

"The idea was discussed. With the hunters drawing on federal resources it was deemed a bad idea, considering there aren't many tech geeks among the magician community and we couldn't ensure call security."

I nodded. There weren't any magician tech geeks that I'd been able to find, either. We wanted more magicians as our roadies when we were on tour, so we could rely on discretion in case a magical mishap occurred. But nope, not so much. Bummer.

"The Titania and Oberon are negotiating a temporary travel pass through Faerie for those of us who can't shadow-step at the moment."

"You think that'll work?" I asked.

"Possibly." He grimaced. "Though the faerie council is

chafing at all the changes we've asked them for since we discovered the demon/hunter problem. Immortal beings are resistant to change."

"I bet." I peered up at him. "I feel like our fans know more about the status of our relationship than we do."

"True. We haven't had much time to discuss what we want out of being soul mates."

"To be honest, I'm still processing the whole end of the world thing." Hell, a good chunk of my emotional energy was tied up in processing being away from my haunted mansion and exposed to new people. My safe, solitary routine had been ripped away and replaced with a strange cast of magical characters.

Zach caressed my cheek, his expression soft with the look of a man who was pondering a kiss. Before our lips could meet, we were rudely interrupted by the appearance of Portia Silverleaf, frost faerie punk princess.

"They said yes," she announced. "Let's go, fang face. Chop chop!"

We sighed in unison. The dogs might love her, but I was creeping toward the urge to slap a bitch.

"Thank you, Lady Silverleaf." Zach stepped back and squeezed my hands once more. "Are you ready?"

Nope. Not even in the slightest. But I nodded dutifully because there was no avoiding this meeting. I wasn't wearing war council attire, but I was all out of fucks to give. They could deal with rumpled Ivy in a hoodie and jeans.

That must have been enough for Portia because we were teleported to a boring undisclosed location inside a dimly lit cinderblock room with a circle of folding chairs that looked suspiciously like an AA meeting in a church basement. The air was stale with a hint of damp and mildew, and I glanced around for a folding table offering coffee and day-old donuts.

I'd been participating in virtual meetings since my self-imposed exile.

My name is Ivy, and I'm an addict.

I edged closer to Zach and took his arm. I hadn't slipped on my cast-iron bitch lead singer persona since the attack, and I felt awkward around new people without my Poison Apples armor. The assembled magicians weren't entirely comprised of wealthy white people, which was somewhat surprising. The magician population was a small percentage of modern society, thanks to centuries of witch hunts that killed magicians indiscriminately, and outright state-sanctioned genocide against indigenous magicians.

Zach showed me to a chair and then dragged one over to sit beside me. The rest of the participants took their seats, their entourages behind them. I assumed Zach's uncle Faust would be sitting with us, but instead he had his own spot with Patience, who was apparently representing the summoners by herself because the rest of the local summoner population was either dead or missing in action. That had to be a hell of a story. From my experience with Jorge, I knew that summoners were tough bastards—the faint of heart didn't last long when dealing with demons. The band instigated a strict "no summoning while on tour" rule after a traumatic incident with a succubus.

Once introductions were done, Catherine Duquesne waved in my direction. "Councilman Harrison and Miss Taylor were attacked last night by a team of hunters. Please describe what happened."

"You're a councilman?" I asked Zach, voice low.

"Did I not mention that?"

"No you fucking did not."

Councils of Three arbitrated magician disputes, starting at local levels like a city council and going up to regional, national and so on. My stomach dropped as I realized what council Zach had to be on—the necromancer council. Son of a bitch. It was bad enough that my soul mate was a fucking vampire, but this meant he was also a *politically important* fucking vampire.

This was bullshit and I did not like it.

I folded my arms and glared at him. "Go ahead. Talk, politician."

Zach launched into the story, and I did not correct him when it came time to describe how the demons were taken care of and let him give Helen the credit. From what I understood about Helen, I doubted that she'd be welcome if she decided to pop in for a chat with the council.

I eyed the gathered crowd while Zach spoke, and estimated just how screwed I'd be if these people knew what I really was. If I hadn't met Zach before I probably would've fried him on the spot when he came calling at my haunted mansion. I reached up and felt for my necklace in reflex, but I'd left it safe at home. (Home? Was Zach's place home now?)

There were several damn good reasons why tempests were extinct. Chief among them was the fact that many tempests cracked under the pressure of so much power at their fingertips. To be honest, climate change had been increasingly messing with me for years. One hundred-year floods every year? Massive hurricanes? Swarms of tornadoes? Yeah, that was like giving an addict the good shit, and I knew I was an addict. A little less self-control on my part and I could do massive damage to unsuspecting people for several miles around me.

Or to the hunters, I supposed. Telling Zach might not be the worst idea if he swore not to share that information.

The second important reason that tempests are extinct was the fact that they were in high demand as weapons to be wielded by other magicians. Rather like seers, who were on the endangered species list thanks to Old World magicians fighting over them like ravenous dogs with a bone. Everyone wanted their own tempest to point and shoot at their enemies. By the amount of council members who eyed me like I had *Milkbone* stamped across my forehead, there'd be a queue forming if it let slip that I had enormous power at my fingertips in addition to fame and fortune.

Zach gently touched my shoulder—apparently I'd missed something. "Sorry? I kind of zoned out there. Been a crazy couple of days."

He nodded. "The council wanted to know if you had any additional description of the demons?"

"Big? Scary? Evil?" I shrugged. "I've never seen one before, so I don't have a basis for comparison."

"I can show you a few," Patience said.

I held up my hands. "Please, no. I'm all full up on nightmare material here."

"Oh, honey. You have no idea." Patience's tone was snarky but her fiery wings drooped—she must've been exhausted, trying to hold back the demonic tide. Nati reached over and squeezed her shoulder in a show of support.

"I could read you," a blonde woman across the circle offered. Right, she was the seer, Anne Williams. Both her sweetie and mine bristled at the idea.

"No thanks." I pointed to my head. "It's a hot mess up in here. No need to spread that."

"Oh?" Catherine cocked an eyebrow.

"You know, all artists are a little mad. Fine line between genius and madness, that sort of sh—thing."

One of the vampires nearby—necromancer councilman, right, don't offend the fang-face—shifted and studied me with thinly veiled disgust. "I have heard some of your music, Miss Taylor. It is far from genius."

Zach growled—honest-to-powers growled! I grabbed his arm before he could challenge the guy to a duel or something equally macho and stupid.

I squinted at the councilman. "Wait, are you that guy from *Rolling Stone*? They hated our last album. Every album, to be honest. Hasn't hurt our sales, though." I shrugged, and then grabbed Zach's hand and held it in my lap before he decided to hiss at the dude or something.

Portia Silverleaf jumped up from her seat behind the Duquesnes. "Oh! Oh! He's being naughty again. Can I pull off his other arm?"

I choked and my eyes widened. *What the fuck?*

"No." Lex sighed, as though tired of answering that question.

"Focus, people." Catherine snapped her fingers to get everyone's attention. "Let's move on. There's been no movement on the faerie front, so we need to consider alternatives."

"Faerie front?" I asked Zach, voice low.

"We're trying to get the faeries to fight alongside us," he said. "If they dissolved the Faerie realm, the infusion of magic to our world would give us enough of a power boost to shut the doors to the hell realms permanently."

I nodded—I understood why the faeries would be hesitant about that. Humanity had caused the extinction of several magical races and species, like elves, the poor bastards. Judging by the number of species that went extinct each day due to the parade of fuckups that humanity inflicted on the natural world, it was clear that their track record had not improved.

The faeries had noped out of our world to save themselves. Clocking back in would almost certainly restart their path to extinction.

In sum, the end times sucked for everybody.

Patience cleared her throat. "My team has been collecting research from the few summoner libraries that weren't incinerated. With the help of the Order of St. Jerome, we hope to construct a ritual that will allow us to close the rifts ourselves."

"Define 'we'," the cranky vampire councilman said.

"Not you," she said. "Your dusty ass is not invited. We're thinking of channeling the combined power of all the soul mates in attendance, like a superpowered Care Bear stare to fry the forces of evil."

Zach frowned, and I patted his hand. Guess his privileged childhood had not included Saturday morning cartoons.

"How many soul mates are we talking?" I asked, curious.

"Raise your hand if you have a soul mate," Patience said.

Zach and I raised our hands as instructed, and I blinked in surprise at the number of people who raised their hands. Holy shit. Soul mates were supposed to be super rare, but more than half of the attendees raised their hands. Catherine and Lex Duquesne, Patience and Faust, Nati and Cris, the two shapeshifter council members, Anne Williams and her companion, two of the members of the Order of St. Jerome— wait, no, three. Four? I pinched the bridge of my nose. It would be so helpful if everyone had a "Hello, My Name Is" sticker.

Whatever, their names weren't important. What was important was that this was an unprecedented number of soul mates in the same place at the same time, during an also unprecedented impending demon invasion. It meant something. I had no idea what, because I'm not a seer, but I wondered what the resident seer had to say about it.

I leaned closer to Zach. "Am I allowed to talk to the seer?"

He winced. "You are, yes."

My brow rose. "You did something stupid, didn't you?"

"Several somethings." Zach nodded. "A series of poor life choices, as the Titania would say."

"Right." I cleared my throat and addressed Patience. "So, your master plan is true love conquers all?"

"In a nutshell." Patience grinned.

Yeah, we were all gonna die. I turned to the Titania. "And there's nothing we can offer to the faeries to sway them toward saving our asses? Anything we have that they don't?"

Patience snorted. "Children."

I frowned and tried to think of the appropriate horrifying fairy tale. "Like Rumpelstiltskin?"

"No," Catherine huffed.

"Yes," Portia said. The assembled group turned toward her in shared horror. "What?"

"Faeries have been stealing children?" Catherine appeared a little green about the gills—considering the topic, I would be, too, if I were sporting a baby bump.

Oh no. Were vampires fertile? Did Zach want kids? Tiny bundles of fanged joy? Geez, talk about a breastfeeding nightmare.

Portia folded her arms. "First, Rumpel *bargained* for the child, that's different. Second, we prefer to call them foundlings, because we *find* them. It's hardly our fault when children wander off and find themselves in Faerie."

Oh, this shit needed to be in a song. I could even work that one Yeats poem that Paz liked into the lyrics, how did it go? *Come away, O human child! To the waters and the wild, with a faery, hand in hand, For the world's more full of weeping than you can understand.*

Super on brand, perfect! I patted my pockets for my

phone to take notes, but it was missing, damn it. I didn't even have my lyrics notebook on me—shit, I really hoped it was with my bags back at Zach's home for endangered magicians.

Faust cleared his throat. "My lovely wife was referring to the faeries' desire for biological children, and please do not give voice to the statement that is doubtless simmering in your thoughts, Mrs. Black."

I returned my attention to Zach. "Old argument?"

"Extremely."

Huh. I assumed that the problem in question was that faeries couldn't conceive full-blooded faerie children, hence the reason why so many magicians, myself included, had fractions of faerie heritage in their DNA.

"Are we going to accomplish anything here or can we go home?" I asked. "I predict at least a dozen panicked messages waiting for me from my PR people."

He nodded and cleared his throat. "If we are finished with new business, is there anything else that needs to be addressed?"

"No," Anne said. I guess a seer would know.

"Then I ask that this meeting be adjourned," Zach said.

Several attendees grumbled in agreement—guess no one wanted to rehash that particular argument, strange as it may be. Portia was our ride home, but she hung back as we were approached by Anne and her extended entourage. Zach stiffened and I looped my arm through his to present a united front.

"Let me guess, you want autographs?" I smirked.

Anne's expression brightened. "Yes!" Someone cleared their throat and she sobered. "And to hear how you're feeling."

"Me? I'm fine, just some scrapes and bruises. I'm more of an attack-from-a-distance person. Zach's the one who went toe-to-toe with the demons. It was impressive in a very terrifying way." I gently patted his arm and smiled up at him. "Maybe you should consider attacking from a distance, too. I have some genius demon-fighting ideas inspired by classic '80s horror films."

"Holy water in a Super Soaker?" Anne asked.

"More like a potion in a Super Soaker, but yes, you've got the idea." We grinned at each other and ignored the silent alpha male stare down that was happening between our respective soul mates. I turned to Zach. "You can still brew potions, right, hon?"

The "hon" worked as intended and interrupted the testosterone battle. "I don't often, but I have the ability."

"Great," I said. "Ooh, maybe potion grenades, that would work too."

The guardian with the long pink hair—apparently she was Marie Duquesne, Lex's sister—piped up from nearby. "I love spell grenades, they're so useful."

Thus began an all-women discussion of magical weapons and finding wacky, horror/comedy ways to apply them that was quickly joined by Patience and Portia, and even Catherine seemed grudgingly interested. She carried a sword so it seemed like unique weaponry was within her wheelhouse.

Eventually we were all whisked back to our respective homes. Zach and I were returned to my suite and I grabbed my phone and groaned at the number of missed calls. Before I could sort through them, Zach gently touched my shoulder.

"We need to talk."

I snorted. "I don't doubt that, but—"

"I know you're hiding something."

CHAPTER SEVEN

Zach

Ivy froze and I silently cursed myself. I was supposed to be gentle with her, not accusatory, but this was important.

She turned slowly, folded her arms and cocked one green eyebrow in question.

I sighed. "I know Helen didn't defeat those demons. She would be lording her accomplishment over me if she did, and she hasn't said a word about it. Plus she seems to authentically like you, which means you impressed her somehow."

Ivy shrugged slightly. "I'd say I was a hit with the in-laws, but I'm more of a homewrecking hussy than the girl you bring home to meet the parents. Runs in my family."

I frowned. I'd run a background check on Ivy after Miss Williams confirmed the identity of my soul mate. No father was listed on her birth certificate, and her mother was arrested several times for solicitation and drug possession until she finally died of an overdose when Ivy was sixteen.

"You banished those demons," I said.

Her chin tilted. "I did."

"How?"

She rolled her eyes. "Magic."

I did my best to breathe through a bout of temper. After all the sanctimonious lecturing I'd endured about the importance of being honest with my soul mate, Ivy was hiding things from me.

You could make her talk...

No, absolutely not. She had several reasons to distrust me—solid reasons that were worthy of my respect. I needed to prove to Ivy that I was worthy of her trust. The problem was that honesty was a policy I had little experience with—you had to be a master of deception to survive in necromancer politics. Before that, I'd been an alchemist, and alchemist magic focused on altering perceptions and changing outcomes.

Ivy cocked her head. "Why do you assume I'm less powerful than you are? It'd be kind of assholish of the high powers to match us with a large imbalance in magical abilities."

"All signs point to the higher powers being assholes."

Ivy laughed. "True. My point is, just because I came from poverty doesn't mean I'm weaker than some sorcerer prick with a purebred pedigree and a high rank in one of their old boys' clubs. I can throw down when I need to. I just..." Ivy trailed off and stroked the side of her throat. "My stalker got the drop on us. We were distracted, and that put us off-balance."

"Distracted how?"

Her expression saddened and she slumped into the chair behind her. "It was my fault. I got Nick killed. I got caught up in the romance of it all—handsome guardian bodyguard, shielding me from danger. We had chemistry. I should've left him alone, concentrated on what was really important, but I was still—" Ivy broke off with a grimace.

I eased into the seat across from her. "Still an addict?"

"Of anything that might give me a high. In this case it was fear and adrenaline. And, well, sex, drugs, and rock-and-roll."

My hands clenched into fists beneath the table and I fought to keep my expression neutral through a wave of jealous anger. Ivy wasn't mine—not then and not now. Master necromancers were possessive and territorial as a rule, and it was a difficult mindset to break. I was in the process of unlearning everything Laura had taught me, exchanging toxic behaviors for healthy ones. My therapist was a saint, I really ought to up his fee. The whole process would've been hard enough without impending doom looming over everything.

"Will you be safe if you go on tour again?" I asked.

"There'll need to be some changes." She shrugged and waved a dismissive hand. "Provided we don't get slaughtered by demons."

"Spar with me."

Ivy blinked. "Huh?"

"There are going to be more battles in our future. I'd like to see how you fight. It'll allow us to work together cohesively, and I'll have a better idea of your best role in battle."

"Battle." She snorted. "Sounds like a video game. One of those old school arcade games that no one could win without using spending a fortune in quarters." My brow furrowed, and she rolled her eyes. "Lord and Lady, you didn't even play *Mortal Kombat*? What's the point of being a rich kid if you could afford all the expensive toys?"

"I had an unconventional upbringing."

"Uh huh. Between you and me we're going to corner the market on therapy." She rose and wiped her palms on her jeans. "One magical ass-kicking, coming right up."

I grinned. "I'll go easy on you."

Something sparked behind her stormcloud-colored eyes as she smirked. "Oh, honey. You have no idea."

~

Ivy

We moved to Zach's gym. I'd been expecting something more along the lines of a hardwood basketball court, or a weight room filled with machines that resembled medieval torture devices. Instead, we arrived at a concrete room with ominous scorch marks.

"What's with the fire?" I asked.

"I'm half fire faerie. Helen was part of the Infernus clan before they were exiled." Zach shucked his business casual suit jacket and hung it on a peg near the door. "I have unusual abilities for an alchemist or a master necromancer."

His button-down shirt joined the jacket, leaving Zach in only his undershirt, and I took a moment to admire the lean muscles of his bare arms. I'd been up close and personal with every inch of his skin during our Vegas sexcapades, and he was built for a businessman.

"Fire and ice? This is gonna be messy. Hope you have good drainage in this room."

"We do, for the fire suppression system."

Oh, good. I didn't want to be complicit in burning down the mansion or flooding the basement.

I shed my hoodie and hung it next to Zach's jacket, which left me in a black T-shirt with my trademark phrase in bright green font.

My words are poison.

It had sort of become a self-fulfilling prophecy. With the

exception of my bandmates, all my relationships ended in ruin.

Zach removed his shoes and socks, which I suppose made sense, because his shiny oxfords had to have zero traction with those soles. I was fine in my ancient Doc Martens—the soles were worn but should still work on the rough concrete floor. I undid my messy bun and switched to a tight braid instead. If he threw fire, I wanted to make sure that he didn't burn my hair off.

We faced off in the center of the room and it took all my willpower not to bust out Hamilton's ten duel commandments.

"No biting," I said. "No claws. Grappling is okay, but if you draw blood with your sharp, pointy master necro-ness, I will knee you in the groin."

"Agreed. I ask the same for your sharp, pointy ice magic. Please don't impale me." He smirked and my smile sharpened.

"What's the matter, handsome? Don't like bottoming anymore?"

His eyes widened and I took advantage of his stunned moment. I embraced the winter weather and consumed its power. A haze of snow and ice surrounded me and I exhaled a puff of frost. I stretched my arms and a wall of ice formed between us and divided the room in half. The ice was a distraction—I didn't have time to reinforce it enough to stop a galloping Staffy mix, much less a vampire. I retreated and kneeled, then slammed my palm against the floor and turned the room into a skating rink.

Zach cursed and crashed through the ice wall just as I shoved off and slid on my ass backward across the ice. I pelted him with conjured snowballs—annoying but damaging only to his pride, like a Midwestern kid being bullied on his way home from school in January. Zach had apparently had enough and hurled a small fireball, meant to singe and not incinerate. I rolled out of the way and replied with a blast of blizzard.

He threw his arms up to protect his face from the ice and wind, and I shoved to my feet and looped around behind him.

"This is kind of fun," I said. "Do I win something when I drop you? New car? Vacay to Hawaii?"

"You're not going to win."

"No?" I tsked as I tossed a ball of ice from hand to hand. "Sounds like someone needs to be taken down a *peg*." I whipped the ball at his head and he stumbled as he dodged. Score one for Team Ice—though it may be considered cheating by reminding him of our weekend of debauchery. Maybe I'd have a T-shirt made up to wear when we finally had to deal with the paparazzi. *I Pegged Zachary Harrison.*

He studied me, head cocked to one side, as I glided around him as effortlessly as though I wore skates instead of boots. I encased my forearms in ice as I moved, upping my defense as I waited for his attack.

"I honestly can't remember the last time I sparred with someone who specialized in ice." Zach winced. "Except for the Silverleafs, who attempt to kill me on occasion."

"Never a good idea to piss off faeries. That's a rookie move." I added a layer of ice over my chest and back, like a knight's breastplate to protect the squishy organs beneath. "Sorcerers are obsessed with fire because it's easy to destroy things with. You can bring down a building with ice, it just takes more finesse."

"Which you possess?" Fire engulfed his hands as he shifted his weight.

"In theory." I shrugged. "I'm an artist. I prefer to create, not destroy."

He hummed in thought, and then he launched himself at me with supernatural speed.

Fucking vampires. Fear spiked my adrenaline and a storm coursed through my veins as I fought to match his moves with my own. Steam rose in a cloud around us as flames met ice, and my efforts to distract Zach by teasing him backfired as I realized how turned on I was. Arousal and reward were two sides of the same dopamine coin, and my nipples hardened as eager heat pooled in my core.

We fought like partners in a violent tango—I attacked, he defended, and then the roles reversed. The breath huffed from my lungs as my back slammed into a concrete wall. He caged me with his body and I did the only sensible thing I could think of—I grabbed his face with both hands and hauled him down for a messy kiss, the kind that's all lips, teeth and desperation.

Zach groaned, and I braced my hands on his shoulders and hopped up to wrap my legs around his waist. He cursed and shifted to grip my ass as my hips ground against him.

"Please tell me you won't be using this method on the demons." Zach murmured the comment against my mouth, and I laughed.

"Pretty sure it wouldn't work. Unless it was an incubus. This would totally work on an incubus."

Zach growled and it was stupidly sexy. *Damn it, Ivy. Don't taunt the jealous vampire.*

Jealous vampire *soul mate.* Stupid attraction seemed like it was part of the soul mate package. My skin flushed as I realized the depth of my need for Zach—I hadn't had sex since the incident. No flings, no partners and now I had the man who'd rocked my world in the most fabulous, sexually debauched weekend of my life right in front of me. *All mine.* I wanted to strip him down and ride him right then and there, no matter how much we'd regret getting busy on a concrete floor after the fact.

I cried out his name and then found myself on my back, pressed against the ice-covered floor. Steam rose around us like a cheesy dream sequence, but I had zero fucks to give about that as my inhibitions tapped out and left me moaning and writhing beneath him. My back arched as he slid one hand under my shirt, trailed up my torso only to be thwarted by my bra. I'd been cursed—or blessed, if you looked at it from a pop star perspective—with heavy breasts, and no flimsy scrap of ribbons and lace could contain them. The bastard used his fire faerie superpowers to burn through the front of the bra, simultaneously releasing my girls and destroying my T-shirt.

At least he could afford a replacement—heavy duty bras were stupid expensive.

Zach's attention promptly migrated from my lips to my nipples, and I melted into a puddle of *yes, please*. The man had a talented tongue, and I had no arguments. He trailed kisses down my torso until he met the barrier of my jeans, and for one moment our eyes locked as he gazed up my body—

And I promptly freaked the fuck out, because gone were the green-slash-hazel pretty eyes I was accustomed to, and in their place was the pale, frosted shade of a vampire about to strike.

I yelped and shoved him with a gust of winter air as I retreated, shed my ruined clothes and scrambled toward the safety of my hoodie.

No longer topless, I folded my arms and glared at him. Zach crouched, brow furrowed with confusion but eyes still full-on thirsty vamp.

"You promised!" I spat.

"I didn't bite you."

"Your eyes say otherwise." I edged toward the door. "You look like you're a quart low and ready to fill 'er up."

"I would never—"

"Oh, really? Because I'm pretty sure your bitey tendencies are part of the reason why the Oberon looks at you like he'd be happy to relieve your head from your torso."

Zach rubbed his face with his hands, and when he finished his eyes had returned to their normal, human coloring. "I know. I made a mistake—a terrible mistake—and I'm doing my penance for it. I would never bite you without your permission. Expressly given and uncoerced."

Which implied that he'd bitten others before without out their permission, and with coercion. Fuck. My throat tightened—vampires fed on the magic in the blood. It was why they needed magician donors, or prey, and couldn't just grab a straight off the street when they were feeling peckish.

Oh, shit. He'd *know.* Zach would know what I was if he fed from me. He wouldn't buy the ice sorceress story anymore—he'd know something was up. I hadn't had that problem with my stalker because I killed the bastard after he ripped my throat out.

My greatest fear had always been discovery because I was one-of-a-kind, the sort of treasure greedy magicians would kill for. My fingers trailed over my scarred throat, and I took another step away.

"You don't trust me," Zach said.

"We're not there yet. We both have a bucket of issues to work through, and we need to settle down and go to our separate corners to calm down."

He grimaced but nodded. "You're right. I understand. Will you allow me to escort you back to your suite?"

"No, not right now." I fished for my phone in the pocket

of my hoodie to check the time. "You can escort me to dinner later, though."

"Very well."

I retreated before he could say anything else. I needed my dogs. And some fresh air. And a friend. It was definitely time to call the boys.

~

"Dude. That's fucked up."

I rolled my eyes. "Not helpful."

Paz snorted and it sounded like static through my phone's speaker. *"I got nothing on the helpful front. There's no tutorial for your current shitshow."*

I peered up at the second of three helicopters still hovering over Zach's estate and fought down the urge to flip off the cameras. All they were getting at the moment was exciting footage of me tossing the tennis ball for my dogs with a launcher stick while on my phone.

"Face it," Paz said. *"You're a trouble magnet."*

"Sounds like a bad idea for a new song."

Paz's voice softened. *"You know you don't have to stay there, right? You can stay with one of us."*

Yelena dropped a slobbery tennis ball at my feet, and I picked it up and hurled it for her. "I know. I feel like I should work on this soul mate thing, though."

"Think some of that romance mojo might rub off on me? I'd hate to think that Wolfie is my soul mate."

"Fuck you, man," Wolfgang yelled in the background. *"I'm adorable!"*

"Yeah, you are, fuzzball." I turned at the sound of footsteps crunching through the snow and spotted the soul mate in question. "Gotta go, guys. Stay out of trouble."

"We like trouble," Wolfgang said.

I huffed an exasperated laugh. "I know. Talk to you later. Love you."

"We love you too!" The pair practically howled the words before ending the call.

Zach paused beside me and quirked an eyebrow.

"Bandmates," I said. "What's up?"

"The PR teams want us to make a public appearance," Zach said. "They're suggesting a dinner date."

"Isn't that a terrible idea, considering the impending demon doom of it all?"

"Yes, though the hunters won't attack us in the open, or at least they haven't thus far. They've been keeping their actions from the public." He shrugged. "If we can draw the media attention away it will give the others the chance to relocate to another location. If they're seen here, it will raise questions that we don't have answers for."

No kidding. The various magicians in the guest house had no normal reason to associate with Zach. "Where are they going to evacuate to? I thought you were running low on safe spaces, hence your unlikely housemates."

Zach grimaced. "We are. My faerie blooded guests can always retreat to Faerie, but most of us aren't welcome there. We're investigating other safehouse options. Regardless, if we don't give the public something to talk about, they'll storm the gate."

"Right." I knew that all too well from my time on my island of solitude. I frowned in the direction of the front gate. "Do you own a tank capable of driving through that mob?"

The local police had shooed away the fan/media frenzy only for the tide to return a few hours later, louder and more obnoxious.

"I do, after a fashion. Do you have a dinner preference?"

"Is pizza out of the question?"

Natasha dropped her tennis ball at Zach's feet. I gave him the stick and waited to see how he handled the awesome responsibility of Throwing the Ball. He seemed to glom onto the mechanics of the stick right away—insert tennis ball, wind up, pitch. I imagined he'd have to adjust his superhuman vampire strength accordingly, and he did, hurling the ball roughly the same distance I had.

"Oh man." I chuckled as I watched Natasha speed away in pursuit. "That clip is a hundred percent going to be the lead on every gossip show tonight. It's evidence that you've been domesticated."

"Hardly." He kept possession of the stick and threw for Yelena as well. "Pizza is doable, but crowd control will be more difficult."

"Whereas a high-end place will be more discreet, right." I sighed—there went my authentic Chicago-style deep-dish pepperoni. "What are my options?"

"There are a few restaurants downtown, but the traffic adds security problems. There's a place in Wheaton I believe might work. It's a country club, hence a members-only dining experience. It's a Saturday night, so it should have enough of a crowd to spread the word of our attendance to the social media masses." Though I couldn't see it, I could almost hear him roll his eyes behind his dark sunglasses.

Ugh. Country club meant an overabundance of wealthy assholes. I was wealthy, but I wasn't *respectably* wealthy, no matter how many charity functions I arranged. "I don't have anything formal to wear. Or jewelry."

"Patience and Portia have offered to help you with that issue."

Well, that was terrifying. My nose wrinkled. "This is

unfair. All you have to do is put on a suit and look like James Bond."

"Blame the patriarchy," he deadpanned. I threw my head back and laughed, and then I whistled for the dogs.

"All right. You make the arrangements, I'll let the faeries play dress up."

Zach smiled as I relieved him of his stick duties. He caught my free hand and held it. "I apologize for earlier. I'm working on my self-control. I shouldn't have let things go that far."

I squeezed his hand. "Thank you. I get it. You're probably used to partners who've eagerly consented to the blood thing. I just can't. Not now. It's too soon. For that, at least."

"Oh?"

I smirked and reached up to muss his hair, which was a deep gold color in the weak winter sunlight. "Let's give them something to talk about."

With an answering grin he leaned down and kissed me. We didn't have time for a lingering kiss thanks to the two wiggling dogs who desperately wanted more tennis ball time, but it would give the media something to discuss. Vultures. My charity work would be so much easier if I could convince them to cover it with the same fervor that they did my numerous fuckups.

"Dinner will be at eight o'clock," he murmured against my lips.

I sighed. "Can we order pizza in the meantime?"

Zach chuckled and offered me his arm. "Of course."

CHAPTER EIGHT

Ivy

I searched through my luggage for my bag of event makeup—I was sure I'd packed it, even though I hadn't worn any makeup while in my haunted mansion. My equally haunted necklace was currently being guarded by Zach's apprentice Anthony, and Jordan hovered a hairsbreadth above my bedspread, ghostly legs folded beneath her as she observed the goings on.

"She's more of a cool color palate," Portia insisted.

Patience snorted. "This is a media date. She needs to look sizzling, and red and green are complementary colors. That's grade school shit."

I glanced toward my faerie godmothers as they argued over my evening attire—fire and ice. Huh. Guess it was a running theme.

"I thought it was a private club?" Jordan asked me. I wasn't entirely sure if the faeries could see her or not. They were more connected to elemental spirits and not souls of the dead.

"Always assume that TMZ has bugged the room," I muttered in reply.

"What's TMZ?" Portia and Jordan asked in unison.

I glanced back at Patience to encourage her to explain when all hell broke loose. At least this time it wasn't actual hell, and instead of demons the source of conflict was my future mother-in-law. Helen popped into the room in all her Real Housewife glory, Jordan promptly vanished, Portia hissed like an angry snake and Patience grabbed and held her before the frost faerie could throw down with Helen.

I whistled sharply. "Hey! You want to fight, take it to the gym."

Portia growled, a sound so similar to an angry dog that my girls whined, abandoned their dog beds and hightailed it from the room.

"We're going to visit Harvey now," Patience announced. "You kids have fun tonight."

Portia squawked as she was forcibly teleported out of the room, leaving me alone with Helen. She beamed at me, and I fought the urge to step away from her. No point in angering the faerie everyone was agreed was dangerously unstable.

"Hello, darling! Where is your date tonight?"

Darling? The fuck?

I cleared my throat. "A country club in Wheat-something. I don't know the exact details. I'm not from around here and I don't golf. Do people golf in January?"

"Not typically." Helen's head tilted. "I know the place. The mortals there are wealthy, influential, and exceptionally boring. They attend even the off-season because the membership is exclusive and they wish to 'network', though gossip is more like it. I will admit that the food is decent, for mortal fare."

"I know the type. They're ripe for the charity picking,

though." I straightened and put on my *I need donations* smile and launched into my introductory speech. "I sponsor several children's charities on the West Coast and in Nevada, and I plan to expand our programs into the Midwest. Can I count on your support?"

Helen's expression brightened and she clapped her hands like a kid on Christmas morning. "I knew you were *perfect*. You and my Zachary will do such great things together!"

I swallowed the urge to ask just what she had in mind, because I suspect that my idea of great things and hers were radically different. Instead, I cleared my throat. "You've been to this place? You know what kind of attire is appropriate?"

"Absolutely, my dear. Come here, let me get a closer look at you."

I edged closer, and she motioned for me to turn like a designer pondering the right model for a runway show. "I need a high collar, or a scarf maybe. Something to cover my scars."

"Perhaps a lace choker." Helen tapped her chin. "Though I don't advocate hiding them. The scars show that you're a survivor. Unconquerable, like a proper tempest."

I flinched. Shit. She knew. Damn it, of course she knew a tempest when she saw one. Faeries were practically immortal —they could be killed, but it was difficult to do. Most faeries had survived for centuries, maybe even millennia. The older faeries had been around so long that they actually remembered what the elves were like before mankind wiped them out. Tempests had always been rare, but we'd only been believed extinct for a few generations, which was nothing to a faerie. I tried to sputter a reply and she patted my shoulder.

"It's all right, my dear. Your secret is safe with me. I always knew my Zachary would have someone spectacular as his spouse, and I have no intention of placing you in danger of discovery. Now, does your charity portfolio include battered women's shelters? Your scars are a conversation opener for that topic."

I blinked from topic whiplash. While I was glad that she didn't intend to share my secret, did she really just compare my vampire stalker to an abusive partner? My mind took a moment to reboot and I slowly came to terms with the idea. The straight world knew I had a stalker, but not a vampire stalker. It wasn't domestic violence, but I could use the attack to speak out against violence against women.

Well, shit. Helen wasn't just evil, she was an evil genius. I wasn't sure if I should be excited or afraid. Probably both.

"I don't currently," I said. "The main focus is on resources for at-risk children. That's a good idea, though. I'll speak to my non-profit manager in the morning."

"Excellent! Now, you'll need a cocktail dress, not an evening gown. And a wrap of some sort because it's always fucking freezing in that place."

Helen rattled off the list of necessities and I nodded and smiled where appropriate. This was going to be a hell of an evening.

～

Zach

My uncle watched as I paced while waiting for my date, his eyes unreadable behind the smoked lenses of his glasses. Did a PR stunt count as a date? Without the pressure of the media frenzy we certainly wouldn't be leaving the house for dinner considering we were barely a day out from the attack. At least the others would be safe—the Duquesnes had finally agreed that discretion was the better part of valor and were retreating to reside in Castle Silverleaf in Faerie. Michael and Emily Black were joining Dr. Dannaher and Marie Duquesne in a vacation rental out in DeKalb County that Marie had apparently found through an app. Not quite a secure location, but one that the hunters wouldn't anticipate.

Ivy had done well during our spar, but not well enough to convince me that she wasn't hiding something. She was good at reading people—I assumed that all performers must be to some degree—and she used that insight to off balance me and use my distraction as an opening for attack. However, that strategy wouldn't work on one demon, much less two, and though her magic held up against mine it shouldn't have been enough to defeat those demons.

"I shouldn't have to lecture you on how to behave with your soul mate," Faust said. I paused and frowned at him, and he continued, "But your recent track record with women has been poor at best."

"I'm aware." I grimaced. "Poor is being kind. I believe your lovely bride would call it asshole behavior."

"And she would be correct, but I was attempting to be polite. We are family, after all."

"She's still here, isn't she?" I didn't have to say Helen's name, because Faust knew who I was speaking of.

Now it was Faust's turn to grimace. "She won't allow herself to be sent away, not when she knows you've found your soul mate. She's up to something, as usual, but this time I don't know what it is."

"Grandchildren, most likely," I muttered. Helen was a terrible mother, and I didn't have high hopes for her being a decent grandmother.

"Yes, well, we know that won't happen without the intervention of medical science, and we all have enough on our plates with the impending doom approaching."

"No progress on the faerie front?"

Faust sighed. "No. On one hand, I don't want to believe that they're capable of leaving their descendants to be slaughtered. On the other hand, most of them haven't had mortal children in decades, possibly even centuries, and they don't have the same sort of emotional connection as I have to you, or Miss Silverleaf has to Catherine. It's more like..."

"Like the disconnect you had from Simon, believing him dead because you lost track of him?" Simon St. Jerome was one of my least favorite topics, though there was currently a grudging truce between us. We shared the same problem of bigger fish to fry—evil, demonic fish.

"Just so. Our relationship is improving. Slowly. Anne has much to do with that."

I nodded but didn't reply. Anne's seer magic had identified and cured the fractured spell that had been contributing to my toxic behavior, and she confirmed that Ivy was my soul mate. I owed her a debt, but I understood that I needed to keep my distance. I'd behaved terribly toward her.

Our conversation was interrupted by the arrival of Ivy—and Helen. My shoulders pinched with tension and I forced a smile. Ivy appeared unharmed, and she looked radiant.

"Good evening, ladies," Faust said. "Dear sister, are you responsible for Miss Taylor's transformation?"

"I am," Helen confirmed. "I considered it my responsibility since I am familiar with the club and Ivy is my son's soul mate. She looks lovely, doesn't she?"

"Beautiful," I said, and I meant it. She looked much like she had when we first met at her charity auction years ago—sleek, sophisticated and tempting as sin. The black silk cocktail dress hugged her curves, and the off the shoulder straps created a plunging neckline that framed the full breasts I'd briefly appreciated earlier at the end of our spar. The only hint at Ivy's punk rock profession that remained was her green hair, and even that was pinned up in an elegant twist held in place with a jeweled comb.

"Thank you." Ivy smiled and took my arm.

"Are those your diamonds, dear sister?" Faust asked.

I blinked—Helen hoarded sparkling things like a magpie and possessed quite the extensive jewelry collection. I didn't recognize this particular necklace, bracelet and earring set as belonging to my mother, but apparently Faust did. The fact that Helen was willing to share something from her hoard was somewhat terrifying.

Helen cooed at the sight of us. "You look so well together. I'm sure you'll do great things."

Her smile sharpened and I shivered. *Shit.* She was planning something unpleasant. I glanced at Faust and he inclined his head slightly, signaling that he would handle whatever his sister had planned.

Ivy and I spent most of the drive in a conference call with our PR teams. This appearance was only the tip of the media strategy iceberg—we discussed options for which journalist would be the best to sit down with for an exclusive interview and how quickly we could arrange it. Though our combined teams each sounded as though they were one leaked photo away from developing bleeding ulcers, the topic was a refreshing change from the impending demon apocalypse. I was well equipped to handle the media, but saving the world was proving difficult. It seemed as though each victory we managed simply spawned new threats.

Upon our arrival at the club, Ivy stepped out of the car and her performance was flawless. She handled the members as though she was born to old money and polite society. We made the rounds of business contacts and golf "buddies"—I detested the game before I became a master necromancer, and now that I had a sunlight allergy I loathed it even more. I tried to schedule tee times for cloudy days, because some people insisted on conducting business during a round of golf out of some annoying belief that it made these deals more prestigious.

When we finally escaped to our table for dinner, I remembered that we couldn't discuss any of our magician problems, and I struggled to think of an appropriate topic.

"No alcohol, please," Ivy told our waiter. "Though if you could put some unsweetened iced tea in a whiskey glass, on the rocks, that would be awesome." She smiled, and the poor kid blushed. He struck me as the "working his way through college" sort—big dreams, small budget.

"And you, sir?"

I couldn't very well order wine and partake of it without her, so I nodded. "The same, please."

The waiter left and Ivy smiled, a faint twitch of her lips. "I guess it's going to be more difficult avoiding my former vices now that I'm out in the world again."

"I'm sorry, I didn't think—"

"Not your fault." She picked up the ice water and sipped it. "I inherited addiction issues from my mother."

"She passed away?" Her mother's unfortunate fate had been mentioned in Ivy's file, but it was polite to ask instead of inform Ivy that I'd run a background check on her.

"Overdosed, when I was sixteen." Ivy shrugged. "I'd been the parent for years by that point, because she couldn't handle accomplishing anything other than turning tricks and getting high."

"I'm sorry."

"Again, not your fault." She glanced at the diners crowing the room, each eager to be noticed and appreciated by their peers. "We were invisible to these good people, but when they deigned to notice us we were nuisances at best and drains on society at worst."

I swallowed another apology. "What can I do?"

"Do better. Lead by example. Support programs are needed, but they treat symptoms, not the disease." Ivy leaned back and waved the topic away. "That's a discussion for another time."

Our drinks arrived and she thanked the waiter by name. I hadn't bothered to take note of it and I silently scolded myself—I was usually better about such details. We ordered our meals and were left alone again.

"Are you happy?" Ivy asked. "Do you enjoy your work?"

Startled, my posture stiffened in reflex. The memory of my mother's voice whispered through my thoughts. *"Don't slouch, Zachary. Good posture is a hallmark of good breeding."* Now that I was participating in therapy, I realized just how much of my life's path had been chosen by others, a pattern that began long before I met Laura, my necromancer mentor.

"Work is work," I said. "I enjoy being successful at it."

"Is it what you wanted to do with your life? Or did your parents pick the real estate thing?"

"My father did. He could talk for hours about the importance of owning property, which I assume he learned from his father. You've met my mother. She's..."

"Unique," Ivy said. "Right. If I asked six-year-old Zach what he wanted to be when he grew up, what answer would I get? Fireman? Astronaut? Chemist?" She smirked and I chuckled. Admittedly, my mother was disappointed that I'd been born an alchemist and not a sorcerer or summoner—who were generally considered to be the two most powerful breeds of magician—but she grew to appreciate what a talented alchemist could accomplish with the right potions.

"To be honest, I don't remember. I don't think it ever occurred to me that I had a choice."

"Now that is downright sad."

My chest tightened with anxiety, and I focused on taking deep, even breaths—technically master necromancers didn't need to breathe, but the body continued it anyway as an ingrained reflex. It was sad, wasn't it? My entire life had been structured according to someone else's expectations, and aside from a few small teenage rebellions I'd complied with their wishes. Under normal circumstances I could console myself that as a master necromancer the rest of my life would be measured in centuries, and I had plenty of time to pursue new dreams. Unfortunately, the demons had other plans, and the rest of my life might very well be measured in days.

Perhaps it was time for a midlife crisis—an unlife crisis?

"Six-year-old Ivy wanted to be a teacher. Probably because my teachers were the only positive role models in my life. Then I had this amazing music teacher in third grade, and all I wanted to do in life was to be a musician. Piano, guitar, singer, songwriter." She smiled and glanced away, as though surveying the view of the snow-covered grounds through the window. Her palms flattened on the tabletop, and I realized she was fighting the urge to touch her scars.

"Do you want to go on tour again?" I asked.

"Maybe." She folded her hands in her lap. "First, I need to get the guys together to record a new album. If my voice can make it through that, we'll try a few smaller venues to see how well it holds up to a full concert." Ivy tilted her head and studied me with an impish grin. "You should come on tour with us. You can be a roadie."

"A what?" I frowned, and she laughed. Her laughter was beautiful, I needed to find a way to hear it more often.

"You ever been on a road trip? Cross country?"

"No. If I need to travel that far, I fly."

Ivy wrinkled her nose. "That's boring as hell. Tell you what. If I go on tour, you're coming with. I'll get a tour bus with blackout windows just for us and save you the ordeal of bunking with the boys, though that is part of the experience. See the country—the world if we do a tour with the works. Stop at all the tourist traps. Eat at truck stops and diners and cafes in Small Town, USA. We'll get you a set of world tour T-shirts and cheap jeans."

My brow furrowed as I tried to picture the appeal of such a trip, and Ivy laughed again at my perplexed expression. Provided we stopped the demon invasion, my schedule was flexible. I could leave the business in the hands of my associates and take any mandatory calls on the road. The difficult part would be living as a master necromancer in such a situation. I could stand a limited amount of sunlight, but feeding would be the difficult part. If I brought Anthony with to donate, and perhaps a magician friend of his, it could be feasible. And it would likely make me the best mentor of all time, taking my college-age apprentice on a rock band's world tour.

I was sure Ivy wouldn't allow me to feed from her, and I wouldn't dare ask.

"One step at a time," I said. "You'll have to compose your new album first."

Well, we needed to prevent the demon apocalypse first. Everything else could follow if we survived.

～

Ivy

Dinner was surprisingly pleasant. I expected a return trip to Zach's mansion, but instead his driver left without us as a diversion, and we hitched a ride with a business associate and his partner to Zach's tower in downtown Chicago. They were a lovely couple who were thrilled to be part of our clandestine escape from the media, and I signed autographs for both, much to Zach's amusement.

I expected to be whisked away to a fancy penthouse apartment—which he did have, but that was mainly for appearances, he explained as the elevator descended. Zach really lived in his lair—a ridiculous term that reminded me of the boys playing fantasy video games on the tour bus—located beneath the tower. I peered at the décor when we arrived and snorted—affluent American bachelor pad, but it had far more personality than his mansion did.

"Nice place. You bring all the girls here?"

"No. You would be the third."

"Really? Who was the first?"

"Laura." He cleared his throat with a pained expression. "Catherine Duquesne was the second. She wasn't married at the time."

"But isn't her husband her soul mate?"

"Yes, though they weren't together at the time."

Right. I needed more of that story. The Duquesnes seemed solid in their relationship. If they knew they were soul mates then and they weren't together there was a reason, and I suspected that said reason was part of the motivation behind Lex Duquesne's resting murder face when he and Zach were in the same room.

"Do you have something I can wear?" I asked. "Workout clothes, maybe? Then we're going to eat ice cream and you're going to tell me that whole sordid tale."

Zach winced. "I can acquire clothing and ice cream, but

you'll have to do the eating. I've probably already eaten more than I should today."

I quirked an eyebrow. "So you can eat, but you don't need to?"

"I'm physically capable of eating, but it does nothing for me and digestion burns magic. Rather like how I can bear sunlight. Magic heals the damage to my skin, but the longer I'm exposed, the more I risk running out of magical fuel, as it were."

"Noted."

I changed into a set of his workout regalia, which was comically oversized on me, and we settled onto his leather couch.

"The guest house has been evacuated," Zach said. "Anthony and the staff are the only ones left on the grounds, and they've been instructed to call for Faust and Patience in case of emergency."

"Thank the powers." I breathed a sigh of relief—that was one crisis averted. I knew from experience how much damage one paparazzi evading security like a Cold War spy could cause. Fuckers. The last thing we needed was the distraction of a pic of Patience and Portia's wings to show up online while we were trying to cancel the apocalypse.

"Okay," I said. "Start talking." I dug into a pint of butter pecan gelato while Zach launched into the tale of his recent terrible behavior. Other than a few nods and hums of agreement at the appropriate places, I let him talk it out. When he finished he sighed and held his head in his hands, and I set my empty container on the coffee table.

"What does your therapist say?" I asked.

Zach groaned. "He says that I was a victim of Laura's abuse, and while I'm coming to terms with accepting that, I also need to acknowledge that my actions hurt many people.

Finding ways to make amends—not necessarily with the people I've harmed, because I'm not owed their forgiveness—will help my peace of mind and balance my karma."

"You have a witch therapist, don't you?" I asked dryly.

"Witches are healers." The corners of his mouth twitched in a faint smile. "Catherine introduced us. Otherwise, a witch wouldn't have given a master necromancer a second glance."

"You weren't on the necro track before Laura, right?"

"No, I'd never considered it. My mother is immortal, and it hasn't done her any favors."

"Are you happy being this?"

"I thought I was." Zach grimaced and looked away, as though he was intently studying the coffee table's wood grain.

Huh. Was my soul mate also unhappy with the fact that he was a vampire? Lord and Lady, weren't we a pair? The corners of my mouth twitched as I fought a wry smile. We were both broken in our own unique ways, but we could face those issues together. I scooted over to him, straddled his lap and tilted his head to face me.

"Hey. I know it's a lot to carry, but you don't have to carry it alone. Your uncle is supporting you, and you've got me in your corner now. We'll do the Zach and Ivy Redemption Tour together, as a team."

His brows rose, and then he smiled and lightly rested his hands on my hips. "Will there be tour T-shirts?"

"Totally." I grinned and he laughed—Zach had a warm, pleasant laugh, and I wanted to hear it more often. "Seriously, though. I've fucked up a lot of good things in my time. I've been to a lot of therapists, though only the last one stuck. Almost dying really shocks a person onto the straight and narrow."

"Are you going to tell me what you've been hiding?"

I flinched, startled. And here I'd thought I was successful

with my magic on ice performance. "Yes, but not today." I sighed. "I've never told anyone about this. It's 'take my secret to the grave' levels of life threatening."

"But you will tell me?"

Did I want to tell him? On one hand it felt inevitable that I'd have to tell my soul mate my dark secret since the odds were in favor of us being stuck together, but did I trust him with this? I studied him as I composed my answer. He looked so human, vulnerable even. I ran my fingers through his hair and then traced the line of his jaw.

"Why do you think they matched us?" I asked softly. "The higher powers, I mean. Because we're both broken?"

Zach caught my hand and kissed my palm. "Not broken. Scarred, perhaps, but healing."

Healing. Right. In reflex I reached for my throat with my free hand but he caught it, and he gently held both my hands in his. He was warm and I felt the light brush of his breath against my skin—he seemed so alive.

"I don't want to be a necromancer," I said. "I don't want to live forever."

His breath hitched and then he nodded. "I understand."

"Thank you." I leaned in and rested my forehead against his. "I'm going to tell you my secret, I promise, but the last person I trusted on this kind of level was killed in front of me. I'm still recovering from that."

A mischievous glint sparked in Zach's eyes. "If it helps, I'm harder to kill. I'm already mostly dead."

"Noted." I laughed and leaned back. Eager to change the subject, I cocked my head. "How much do you remember about our weekend in Vegas?"

Zach licked his lips and his energy shifted. "I remember more now than I did when I was under Laura's influence. I think that affecting my memory may have been part of the initial spell—everyone else faded away in favor of focusing on her."

"Hmm." My smile turned sly and sultry. "I'll allow it. Otherwise I'd be offended. It was easily in my top ten best sexploits."

His brow furrowed and for a moment I could swear I caught a hint of smoke as jealousy singed his aura. *Idiot, are you really poking the vampire? The same vampire who looked at you like an afternoon snack just a few hours ago?*

Yes, yes I was. I made a note to discuss my poor life choices with my therapist, provided the world didn't end before our next session.

"Top ten?"

I traced his frown lines and subtly shifted my weight in his lap. "Could be top five, depending on the judging criteria."

"Judging criteria," he repeated, his voice flat. His hands tightened on my hips.

"Don't tell me you don't have your own criteria for what constitutes a good fuck."

He growled, and I pressed a finger to his lips as though shushing him.

"No biting. I will stab you."

"It's better with a bite."

"Like it's better with a potion?" I quirked an eyebrow.

"Isn't it?"

"Guess we'll just have to find out if sober sex can live up to the challenge."

He growled again but the sound cut off suddenly as he closed his eyes and inhaled a deep breath. My brow rose, curious, as I watched him rebuild his composure brick by brick. When he opened his eyes again his gaze was heated but controlled. He raised a hand to my face, caressed my cheek and then brushed his thumbs across my lips.

"May I?" Zach asked. My pulse thundered in my ears as I nodded, and he smiled. "Verbal consent, please."

"Yes."

He leaned in for a soft kiss—a gentle, almost hesitant press of his lips against mine that was nothing like the frenzied devouring we'd shared during our spar a few hours earlier. I threaded my hands through his hair and pulled him closer, and I opened my mouth and my tongue flicked against his lips.

The corners of his mouth twitched and amusement glinted in his eyes. "May I?"

I shivered at the heated tone of his voice—who knew that those two simple words could be so sexy? "*Yes.*"

Zach cupped the back of my head and drew me close. He opened his mouth to mine and deepened the kiss, a slow exploration as though he was memorizing the taste and texture of my lips and tongue. I moaned and rocked my hips atop his lap, feeling his hard arousal beneath me. The hand at my hip slid beneath my borrowed shirt and splayed against the small of my back.

"May I?"

"Yes, please."

He gripped the shirt, tugged it over my head and tossed it aside. He deftly unhooked my lacy date bra with one hand—kudos to me for remembering to pack the sexy underwear—and then it joined the shirt somewhere on the floor. His hands spanned my waist, so close to my bare breasts but making no move to touch them. Instead he moaned low as he drank in the sight of me.

"You're so beautiful." His grip slid up, tantalizingly slow, until he stopped just before cupping my breasts. "May I?"

"Yes, damn it." I nearly growled the words as I rocked against him.

Zach teased the bud of one breast, rolling it between his thumb and forefinger while he lowered his head and took the other into his mouth. I leaned back and gasped as the heat pooling in my core pulsed as he teased me with his hands, lips and tongue.

"Harder," I demanded.

Zach hummed against my skin and increased his attentions until I was a panting, writhing mess.

"Tell me what you want," he said. "Please, Ivy."

"I want you to take me to bed." I nibbled his bottom lip with a hungry smile. "I want you to kiss every inch of my body. I want you to make me come with your mouth and your hands before I take your cock, and then I want you to fuck me until I collapse."

Zach grinned. "As you wish."

CHAPTER NINE

Ivy

I woke to an empty bed and the scents of bacon, coffee and maple syrup. I frowned as my brain lurched toward being completely awake, and the fact that I felt pleasantly sore and well ravished brought me up to speed on where I was and what happened.

I found another set of Zach's comfy workout clothes neatly folded on the nightstand, and I dressed and went in search of him. A small dining table with two chairs had been set up in the bar area of his bachelor pad. Zach's place was empty of food and instead held a laptop, which he perused with an annoyed expression. I took the empty chair and helped myself to breakfast.

"Yes! Waffles." I grinned and heaped a pile onto my empty plate. "You, sir, are a gentleman and a scholar."

"I was hoping for 'good date,' but I'll accept that compliment." Zach smiled. "How do you feel?"

"Pretty damn awesome if I do say so. Enthusiastic consent may be my new favorite thing. How did our media stunt go?"

I dressed the waffle tower with butter and syrup, and then added bacon to my plate for protein.

"Well. My firm sent highlights of the media response. Your associates likely emailed similar report to you."

I nodded. My phone was in my clutch purse, and my purse was...here somewhere. "Did the detail about the tea in the liquor glasses get out?"

"Surprisingly, no."

"Aww, good kid. We should send him something nice as a thank you."

We chatted about our next steps while I consumed my carb-laden breakfast. For now, we had a window of media-free opportunity considering that they were camped out around the mansion and not the tower. I was tempted to suggest an incognito tour of Chicago—with the right winter attire, we'd be unrecognizable. Scarves, knit caps, sunglasses, puffy coats...

Zach's phone rang and he glanced at the screen. "My PR firm." He answered, and his neutral expression shifted into a deep frown. "When?"

"What happened?" I set my fork down and chugged a fortifying gulp of coffee. I followed as he crossed to the coffee table and snatched the TV remote. He flipped to a news network and my jaw dropped—an aerial view of the mansion, with a convoy of black SUVs that screamed "federal agents" parked in the circular drive.

"The fuck is that?" My hands clenched into fists and I fought down the urge to reach for the power hovering around me. There wasn't a storm to pull from, but there was Lake Michigan, and I could do a lot of damage fueled by the lake.

"That is a complication." He growled a few orders to the unlucky person on the phone about contacting our legal teams, and then he ended the call.

"Define complication."

"The hunters' fake feds issued a search warrant. Some made-up charge about fraud or tax evasion." He pinched the bridge of his nose and winced. "I need to warn Anthony. He needs to evacuate with the magician staff if they haven't already."

"I'll call my people." I frowned and glanced around for my purse. "Okay, first I'll find my phone, then I'll call my people."

In a whirlwind of activity I located my purse, left messages to warn my Poison Apple boys of possible fake men in black, hunted up my underwear and then frowned at the stupid high-heeled shoes. It was either wear them and risk breaking an ankle if we had to book it away from the bad guys or go barefoot ala John McClane and risk fighting demon terrorists with the soles of my feet full of glass.

Damn it. I chose the shoe option with the caveat that I could ditch them if needed.

"Did Anthony and the staff get out okay?" I asked.

Zach nodded. "It took some fast talking on Faust's part to convince the faerie council, but they've all been evacuated to Faerie on a temporary basis."

"But not your mother, I assume."

"No, but she can take care of herself."

"Right. Do you have an evacuation plan for us? I assume the forces of evil are headed here after they realize we're not at the house."

He grinned. "I have an escape tunnel."

"Whoa, no shit? Good work, Bruce Wayne."

True to his word, the man had an honest-to-gods escape tunnel built into his lair behind a secret door worthy of any old school murder mystery. The tunnel itself was more of a utility accessway than a creepy passage, with thick pipes and bundles of cable running along one side of the tunnel. The stale air hummed with the power traveling through the cables and my fingertips tingled with the potential lightning. Zach led and I followed close behind.

"Where does this go? The Bat Cave?"

He chuckled. "No. Parking structure under the building to the south, which I also own. There's a car waiting."

"The Batmobile?"

"I'm not a hero."

I pinched myself to prevent parroting the quote "you either die a hero or live long enough to become the villain" from Christian Bale's run as the Dark Knight. To magician society, Zach was a villain. Had the alchemist version of Zach I'd met years ago died a hero when he became a necromancer? Caught in my inappropriate musing, I collided with Zach when he paused at the end of the tunnel to open the escape hatch.

We emerged into an empty section of a parking garage, and standing between us and a non-descript escape sedan were five demons poorly disguised as white men in black business suits and sunglasses.

Zach cursed under his breath. "The tower wards don't extend far enough to cover this building."

"Oops. Hey, are those the same assholes from my house?"

"If they are, they brought friends."

My magic reached for the leashed lightning in the power cables bundled behind us. "They should have brought more."

The lead demon agent smiled politely and a chill shivered down my spine. "Please come with us. Your compliance will be rewarded."

"That seems unlikely," I said. "You don't strike me as the reward type."

The fake smile widened to an inhuman degree, full of

menace and sharp, white teeth. "We will reward you by not torturing the friends you left behind at the mansion."

Zach snorted. "You didn't capture anyone there. They were gone before you even set foot on the property."

The tension eased in my chest, but then the demon replied, "Perhaps. But Miss Taylor's bandmates were not guarded by faeries, were they?"

The lights overhead flickered as fury roared through me—the boys' phones had gone straight to voicemail. Those *bastards*. They took my boys. I was going to *destroy* them.

"Does it hurt?" I asked.

The demon tilted its head. "Pardon?"

"When you're banished back to the hell you crawled out of," I said. "Does it hurt?"

"Ivy, don't," Zach murmured in warning. I ignored him.

"Because I really think this is going to hurt." I smiled sweetly and called down the thunder—or in this case, the lightning. "Go to hell!"

Lighting burned a hole clean through the chest of the lead demon. It glanced down like a cartoon character who'd just taken a point-blank shotgun blast, and then it melted to the ground in a smoking puddle of black ooze. The remaining demons zoomed forward to attack before I could ready another round. Zach engaged two while I burst a water pipe and directed the flow at my attackers. It knocked the demons back and gave me enough time to form my ice armor.

"Portia!" I called out. "We could use an evac." We couldn't call Faust or Patience for backup because there were bound to be more demons waiting in the shadow realm. We needed to escape to Faerie, provided that the faeries would continue to bend the rules and grant Zach entrance.

A demon charged and tried to grab me, and then it howled in pain and frustration as ice spikes sprang from my forearms. I hauled back to punch the jerk, but one of the demons Zach was fighting stumbled into me and knocked me off my heels.

Fucking high heels. I was writing a strongly worded email about client safety to Balenciaga after this.

I fell and hissed at the impact of my knees colliding with concrete. My opponent used the opportunity to strike at my head—which was not armored, because apparently my vanity had considered an ice helmet dorky. I yelped as my skull throbbed with pain and momentarily scrambled my brains. I rolled away from a second hit and squinted up at the demons. Water from the broken pipe seeped through my borrowed clothes as a puddle spread across the parking deck.

"Zach! Get clear!"

I gave him a moment to flee, and then I channeled lightning and used the water as a conductor to fry the fuckers. And myself, too, but my magic didn't hurt me too much. Just felt like a monster shock of static electricity, which I could deal with. More or less. My head felt fuzzy as I blinked up at the concrete ceiling.

I heard Zach call for Portia and then he appeared at my side. "Ivy! Are you okay?"

"Little crispy. Think I have a concussion. Those fucks hit hard."

He scooped me up in a princess carry and sighed in the direction of the car. "They can track us as long as we're outside the wards."

"Go back?"

"They'll just send their fake fed team here to drag us out for a public perp walk."

"And the faeries aren't answering us because...?"

"Because I was busy."

Zach turned and I spotted Portia Silverleaf. I waved halfheartedly. "I have a concussion. Can we get ported somewhere nice? Like Hawaii?

Portia cocked a thin white eyebrow. "They'll find you there, too."

"The Vatican?"

"Please, no," Zach said.

Portia snorted. "Hang on, you're cleared for access to Faerie. I'll take you to the others."

We popped out of the parking garage and into a room filled with members of the pan-magician council. Or at least the members with soul mates. Huh. Weird.

"Catherine." Zach set me down on someone's couch. "Ivy took a blow to the head. I think she may have a skull fracture."

"I fine. I fuzzy."

"Yeah, that doesn't sound like fine to me." Catherine sat beside me and did some sort of witch healer's diagnostic and frowned. She motioned for someone out of my line of sight and they pressed a coffee mug into my hands. "Drink that."

I glanced down at the mug's bright pink contents. "The fuck?"

"It's good for you," she said.

"Looks like unicorn piss."

Portia bounded into view. "Lord and Lady, someone finally figured it out!"

A chorus of *what*s sounded throughout the room. Deciding that I'd done worse in my time, I cautiously sipped the liquid and took notes on the commentary around me for future ridiculous song purposes.

"Why do you think it's so rare?" Portia folded her arms as people around me voiced their horror.

"You're not serious."

"What is this, I don't even—"

"For fuck's sake—"

My head cleared a fraction after each sip. Catherine walked away to join the collective freakout and Zach helped himself to her spot on the couch. Though couch might be something of a misnomer—it was probably a divan or something equally fancy, upholstered with thick midnight blue fabric embroidered with intricate silver snowflakes and frosted leaves.

"We need to talk," he murmured.

"Not now. Brain is healing." I leaned against him and he turned, wrapped his arms around me and pulled me against his chest.

When the cacophony died down the topic turned to "oh shit, what do we do now?"

"Don't suppose that because we all got a free pass to come here means that the faerie council is down with our plan?" I asked.

"Not as such, no," Lex drawled. "This was more along the lines of they'd feel bad if we all died."

"Aww, they like us," I said. Several dry laughs echoed in reply. Feeling steadier, and with my vision in focus again, I scanned the room. It was a soul mate convention up in here.

"Hey, Portia," I said. "Can someone check on my band members?"

She nodded. "Riley and Jere's cousins are taking care of it, which means they'll probably be teleported to their respective territories and then brought here."

Riley and Jere being the weretiger soul mates who represented the shapeshifters on the pan-magician council. I hadn't had a chance to speak with them yet, and I had questions about weretigers. Wolfgang was a wolf shifter, which was basic as hell and I wanted to know just how extra weretigers were.

"Where is here, for the record?" Zach asked.

"Castle Silverleaf. You're welcome."

Whoa. I craned my neck to take in more details of the room, wondering what a real faerie castle looked like. I doubted that Tinkerbell zipped around the towers every night and fireworks burst overhead, but it did have a Disney-esque feel thanks to the mix of medieval architecture with modern comfortable amenities. Stone walls without the accompanying drafts, and wide, tall stained-glass windows that might look at home in a cathedral but wouldn't repel an invading army.

"Why the change in tactics?" I blurted. Someone was going to have to relieve me of the unicorn piss soon because I was teetering on the edge of intoxication, and I didn't want to lose my sobriety streak.

As though hearing my thoughts—soul mate telepathy, maybe—Zach gently took the mug and set it on a side table.

Lex Duquesne grimaced. "They might've changed the timetable for their invasion."

"Team Banishment hasn't seen any evidence of that." Patience folded her arms and steam hissed around her fiery wings.

Banishment. Something about the word struck me funny, and then my stomach sank. Oh no. The demons I fried weren't dead, they'd just been sent home. They had to know something was up with my magical skill set.

I continued my non sequitur train. "How old do you think the demons we've been facing are? Like on a scale of just graduated college to used to run with the dinosaurs?"

Patience smirked. "I'm thinking centuries more than millennia for most of them. Why?"

Centuries was long enough to remember the tempests. I

swallowed hard and leaned harder into Zach's arms. It felt nice, even though everything else had gone to shit.

"Working on a theory," I said. "But I'm still out of sorts. How long does our free pass last? Do we have time for a nap?"

"You shouldn't sleep with a concussion," Catherine warned.

"Shower then? I was just flat on my back in a puddle on the floor of a parking garage and I wasn't even wasted."

Portia's nose wrinkled. "Gross. Well, you'll be our guests for a few days, at least, so we'll get everyone settled into guest rooms. You can reconvene over dinner."

Zach

I changed into clean clothes provided by our faerie hosts. Unlike most alchemists, I'd never been to Faerie, because though I was faerie blooded, my relatives were shadowspawn —faeries who'd been banished for evil acts, their lands forfeit. I knew that my mother was the main culprit in said evil acts, but I'd never pried into the precise details of what happened. Faust was always quick to change the subject, and getting the truth out of Helen was nigh impossible. I wondered what their clan's home had been like. Faeries could change their appearance with a thought, and I'd seen Faust's true form—he was a being of earth and fire, like lava brought to life in a humanoid form. I doubted that the Infernus clan had favored medieval trappings like the Silverleafs did.

The wardrobe in our guest room was filled with clothing in our sizes, but the fashion choices were strange to say the least, ranging from Shakespearean ruffs to parachute pants. I chose the blandest shirt and trousers I could find and that looked the least like they were taken from the wardrobe of the Joffrey Ballet's production of *The Nutcracker*.

I searched for clothes for Ivy while she bathed. She was hiding something—I'd never met a magician who could throw lightning before. That sort of skill was almost unheard of among modern magicians, or among the living ones. It was possible that a few of the elder master necromancers were capable of wielding that kind of magic. Most sorcerers were born aligned with only one element—earth, air, fire, or water. Some were able to combine two, like ice from air and water. I'd witnessed Ivy using air and water, but this?

Whatever secret Ivy guarded, the demons had noticed and would change their plans to capture us accordingly.

I frowned at a ball gown—honestly, the Silverleafs thought we had time for a ball? Then I noticed that my hands were shaking and I took a slow step away from the wardrobe. I hadn't fed since Anthony donated when Ivy and I arrived at my family estate. I'd burned up energy while sparring, and then again while fighting the demons. I needed to feed, and I hadn't seen Anthony when we arrived. I doubted that Portia would leave him behind. Maybe he'd been relegated to the servants' quarters.

For master necromancers, hunger doesn't have the same symptoms as it does for the average human. As unpleasant as it is to contemplate, necromancers are the walking dead, considering that the ritual that creates us freezes our bodies at the moment of death. We're sustained by the magic in the blood we ingest, and as a necromancer's proverbial tank runs low, we become increasingly agitated. A starved vampire is a dangerous, feral thing.

Ivy emerged, wrapped in a towel, and I sighed and waved a hand at the wardrobe in defeat. "There are clothes in our sizes, but the assortment is...eclectic."

"I can handle eclectic. I'm a rock star."

She advanced and I retreated to the other side of the room and found an armchair to slump into. Hunger warred with the old instincts to lose my temper—Ivy was mine, and she was hiding something from me. *She's lying, just like Helen. Just like Laura.*

I covered my face with my hands and tried to channel my therapist and his advice about avoiding toxic thoughts and behavior.

"Are you okay?" Ivy asked. "I got first aid and you didn't. Are you injured?"

"Nothing severe." Though healing my wounds had contributed to my current hunger problem. "What aren't you telling me?"

"That's a loaded question."

I glanced up and she had donned a gray sweater and a long black skirt. She sat on the bench at the end of the bed, and I folded my hands to fight the urge to reach out to her.

"You're hiding something," I said.

"Always."

Fury seared the edges of my mind as my hands twitched. *Exactly like the others. She wants to use you for her own agenda.*

Damn it, no. I was the one who sought Ivy out and dragged her into this mess. She could hardly have an agenda to manipulate me when we had only been together for a handful of days.

I managed a calm reply. "Why?"

She grimaced. "Because it's the kind of secret that magicians would kill for. Did kill for, in the past."

I swallowed a demand that she tell me, followed by an assertion that I had a right to know. The words were bitter and burned like acid in my chest. Instead, I breathed deep and chose a better response. *I could do this. I could be better than the monsters who created me.*

"Please, Ivy. I can't protect you if I don't know why they want you."

"I don't need protection." A wry smiled quirked the corners of her mouth. "But we're partners in this soul mate thing. It was probably inevitable that I'd tell you. The end of the world just escalated the issue." Ivy curled up on the bench and hugged her knees to her chest, the tips of black beaded slippers peeking out from beneath her skirt.

"Please." My pulse thudded as my atrophied heart thumped in my chest.

She nodded and sighed. "I'm not just a sorceress. I'm a tempest."

My brow furrowed as I frowned. "I'm not familiar with that term."

"Most magicians aren't, unless they're librarians or old enough to have lived before tempests went extinct." She peered at me. "Tempests draw on all the elements. We can control the weather, though that's tricky as hell. The butterfly effect, you know? You end a drought in one area and can cause a hurricane in another."

I nodded slowly at the implications—a magician with a tempest on their payroll could cause havoc for their enemies. Unfortunately, I knew just what sort of magicians would covet that kind of power. "Necromancers destroyed your people, didn't they?"

"Along with the major sorcerer houses, and pretty much any magician who hungered for power over others."

"Which is most of them. I wouldn't—damn it. I can't say that I wouldn't want that power under my control. I wanted to control Catherine to gain influence in Faerie. I'm...better now, but I'd be an idiot to claim that I've been cured of my asshole tendencies."

Ivy snorted. "You and me both, honey." She squared her shoulders. "You can't tell anyone. I mean that. I'm trusting you with this, and only you."

"I suspect that my mother knows. It would explain her behavior toward you. She's only pleasant when she's plotting."

"She knows, she already let that slip." Ivy sighed and propped her chin on her knees. "I assume the demons know. Because I Force lightninged them and it banished them instead of killing them. I didn't think about that at the time with the imminent doom and all."

"Force lighting?"

"It's a *Star Wars* reference...fuck a duck, you've never seen *Star Wars*? I am so unleashing Paz on you when he gets here."

"That sounds unpleasant."

"You have no idea. Try being stuck in a tour bus with him in the middle of Kansas while he's on a rant about some Jedi shit." She rolled her eyes. "What's our next move? Meet with the faerie council?"

"Yes, though..." I grimaced—there was no way to say "I need to feed" in this situation without sounding like a monster in a low-production horror movie. "I need to speak with Faust first."

She nodded, and I called for my uncle. He appeared in our room with his bride in tow—who I had specifically not called for.

"How're you feeling?" Patience asked Ivy.

"Like my skull was bounced on the cement like a basketball."

Patience turned to Faust. "Is that pink stuff really unicorn piss?"

Faust shrugged. "I wouldn't know. There were no unicorns

native to my clan's corner of Faerie. The Emerald Willow might know."

"Yeah, no. Beatrice hates my flaming guts." She flexed her fiery wings in emphasis and then turned to me. "What's up, buttercup?"

Lord and Lady. I would be so grateful when we saved the world—or when it ended in demonic doom—and I never needed to interact with Patience again.

"I didn't see Anthony when we arrived," I said. "Is he here?"

Faust shook his head. "I believe he and the others in your employ at the estate were sent to their respective faerie clans."

I nodded, grateful that they were safe though it didn't help my current condition. "I don't suppose our gracious hosts will be supplying blood for their guests on a liquid diet?"

"Absolutely not," Faust said. "The chroniclers have been grudgingly welcomed, but you and I are on extremely thin ice here, if you forgive the poor pun. The Silverleaf clan is still furious over their territory being invaded when Catherine was competing to become Titania."

"We had nothing to do with that," I said.

"But Laura and Dorian did, and Laura was your maker. I am, of course, considered undesirable due to my outcast status. I was only allowed passage due to the work we've done with the Faerie council since this demon mess started." His lips pressed in an annoyed line. "We need to tread lightly."

"What happened to Helen?" Ivy asked. "I assume she wasn't on the approved guest list."

"Correct," Patience said. "I assume she scurried away back to her lair of bleach and Botox."

Faust sighed. "Darling."

Patience batted her lashes. "Yes, sweetie pie?"

Ivy snickered at the exchange, and I leaned back in my chair. The other blood-drinkers had willing donors at hand, though I wondered what Mr. and Mrs. Black would do in this situation. Borrow Anne? They couldn't all feed from her.

Patience and Faust's banter came to a crescendo, and she turned to me. "In sum, you're screwed."

"Thank you for your kind words," I said dryly. "When are we expected at dinner?"

Faust folded his hands. "In three hours."

"Thank you," I said. Faust nodded, collected his bride and vanished.

"Do you think my dogs are here?" Ivy asked.

"Yes. It's most likely that Portia absconded with them. She's very fond of the Duquesnes' pets. She took custody of Catherine's cats."

"What about the ghosts? Anthony has the necklace. Can ghosts travel to Faerie?"

I blinked. "I...honestly don't have the answer to that question. They should be safe as long as the spell is intact."

"Good." She eyed me with a pensive expression. "You're hungry, aren't you?"

"Yes, but I won't harm you," I assured her. "I'll figure something out. I may bargain with Catherine to donate."

"Her hubby will punch you in the face."

"It wouldn't be the first time."

"Maybe you should...I mean, it's a special circumstance and all, so maybe just this once..."

"Ivy, no." I shook my head as I wrestled to control my inner hungry beast. "I promised I wouldn't ask this of you, and I won't."

"Well, technically you're not asking, I'm offering. Or considering offering. We all need to be on our A-games here and you won't be if you're hungry. What if there's another attack?"

I grimaced—I'd like to be able to argue that an attack here would be impossible, but as Faust had just mentioned, it had happened last summer thanks to my former mentor and her idiot boy toy.

"You don't need to go for the throat, right?" Ivy asked. "You could pick a different vein, like a Red Cross donation?"

I groaned at the thought of laying her back upon the bed, settling between her spread legs and feeding from her inner thigh. That was certainly not appropriate behavior for a Red Cross blood drive.

I cleared my throat and managed a weak nod. "The wrist, perhaps, but you don't have to do this. I'll find another option. It's not fair to you to be forced into this situation."

On one hand, I was proud of myself for being polite in my denial and keeping my soul mate's agency at the forefront of this matter. On the other, my mind raced with memories of all the eager, willing donors I'd enjoyed in the past, and my traitorous brain replaced those donors with images of Ivy debauched on pleasure—

I squeezed my eyes shut and tried to breathe through the problem like my therapist instructed, but my not-quite-human nature refused to cooperate with his well-intentioned advice. Then, to add fuel to the bonfire of terrible ideas, I opened my eyes to find Ivy standing before me, reaching for my hands. I swayed forward, instinctively leaning into my soul mate's presence. My jaw clenched as I warred with the hungry desire to *take*—to sweep her into my lap, tilt her head to the side and plunge my fangs into her throat, to drink until she was flushed and pliant from an overload of pleasure.

"It's okay," she said.

I shook my head. "It's not."

"I trust you."

"Ivy, *I* don't trust me right now."

"You won't hurt me."

"Causing harm isn't the issue." I licked my lips and stared up at her, and she flinched the moment my eyes shifted to predator pale. "The things I want to do make our weekend in Vegas seem tame in comparison."

"Oh." Ivy blinked, wide-eyed, and took a hesitant step back.

"Don't run," I warned her. "The hunting instinct will chase you."

"Oh," she repeated. Her mouth pressed into a thin line as she regarded me, but then she eased forward and held out her left arm. "I still trust you. And if you cross a line, I'll zap you with so much lightning you'll look like a cartoon who stuck their finger in a power socket."

Startled, I laughed, and it eased a fraction of the tension crawling beneath my skin. I took her hand and tugged her into my lap, possessed by the need to kiss her before I bit her —most people aren't interested in kissing after the bite, unless they're also a blood drinker.

I framed her face with my hands and claimed her mouth, needy and eager. Lord and Lady, I could almost taste the magic humming in her blood, like the last moment of calm before the break of a storm. Ivy moaned low in her throat, and I tangled my hands in her unbound hair, still damp from her bath. A growl rumbled low in my chest at the reminder of the attack. They could have taken her. The demons could have snatched my soul mate away and done gods knew what with her, and I would've been powerless to prevent it.

This was war, and we were losing. That was unacceptable.

I drew back and she gasped for breath, and I raised her wrist to my lips. My fangs pierced her fair skin and my mind short circuited. *Power.* Ivy's blood held power like I'd never experienced before. Whether it was due to her mysterious tempest nature, our connection as soul mates, or perhaps some forgotten faerie ancestry, Ivy's blood was remarkable. Thankfully, that meant I wouldn't need as much as I would need to drink from an average magician.

Revived, I fought the insatiable instinct to gorge myself and overwhelm Ivy with pleasure. Instead, I kept it simple—a painless bite, and just enough blood to refill my drained batteries. I healed the wound left by my fangs and returned her wrist.

"Are you all right?" I asked.

Her glazed eyes seemed to be focused on a point over my shoulder. I held her hands in mine and gently stroked her skin until the episode ended.

"Better now?"

"Yeah." Her voice was ragged and she cleared her throat before turning her attention to me. "Yeah, I'm okay. I was expecting the worst and my brain kind of spiraled from there. Thank you."

"Me?" I asked, startled. "I'm the one in your debt."

"I don't doubt that you could've crossed so many boundaries, but you didn't." She rose and tugged me to my feet. "Come on, it's power nap time before dinner."

I didn't feel tired—the buzz of her magic was like a triple shot of espresso—but I was happy to comply for the opportunity to hold my soul mate. Ivy led me to the bed and I joined her beneath the thick blankets. I wrapped my arms around her, closed my eyes and breathed in the sharp, clean scent of winter mint that clung to her skin and hair after her shower. What would it be like to fall asleep each day with my soul mate in my arms? I'd had many flings and one-and-done fucks, but never a serious relationship. Even Laura had made it clear that our time together was temporary—master necromancers were unageing, and when one counted time in centuries instead of decades it was rare to spend that time with the same person.

I wanted more time with Ivy, but time was a luxury that was quickly running out.

~

Ivy

I pouted when I awoke from my all-too-short nap. I didn't want to move from the warmth of Zach's embrace, and my sleepy brain struggled to compute the fact that my soul mate was warm because I'd let him drink my blood. My magic fueled that pleasant warmth, and I didn't know how to feel about that. My default reaction would be to freak out, but I'd consented to the bloodletting and the world hadn't ended.

Well, at least not from that.

"Do we have to go to dinner?" I asked. "Does Faerie have delivery? Or drive-throughs?"

Zach chuckled and I felt the huff of his laughter against my hair. "Possibly, but this is our chance to regroup before Catherine addresses the council."

Right. Impending doom. I groaned and reluctantly left the comfort of my lover's arms. I perused the wardrobe again and my inner rock goddess was tempted to wear the most outrageous, Met Gala–worthy ensemble I could compose. In the end I stuck with what I was already wearing, took Zach's arm and marched off to dinner.

The dining hall was the sort of ridiculously formal affair featured in movies about royalty or old money—chandeliers hung overhead, high-backed chairs lined a long table heavily laden with a variety of dishes ranging from pedestrian peasant fare to exotic cuisine. *What the fuck, was that a peacock? Lord and Lady, why?*

Zach steered us over to join Faust, and I sat between my soul mate and his uncle.

No one wanted to eat. Despite the absurd amount and variety of food, no one in our odd group of refugees moved to load up their plates. Everyone seemed shellshocked—we'd all been chased from our homes by the forces of evil, with no idea when or if we'd be able to return.

I hated awkward silences, so I decided to shatter it. "We have a plan, right? A cunning strategy to save the world?"

Catherine sighed, her expression vaguely ill as though fighting a bout of morning sickness—maybe she was, since we were all suffering from magical jet lag. Thanks to Helen's diamond-encrusted wristwatch I knew what time it was in our world, but I wasn't sure what the local time was.

"We're speaking before the Council of Three in a few hours," Catherine said.

"Which one?" I asked.

"The council we answer to," she said.

It wasn't the highest of authorities, but unfortunately it was likely as good as we were going to get. What did the highest political power in Faerie think of all this? We were set to argue on the equivalent of a state level, so what did the faerie feds think? Was there dissention in the ranks?

"Are there other Titanias and Oberons arguing with their councils too?" I asked.

"Yes." Lex grimaced, but then he began filling his wife's plate with what appeared to be French fries.

Right then. Might as well refuel since I'd just—my train of thought derailed again at the reminder that I'd let Zach drink my blood. Having a vampire soul mate hadn't quite hit home when I'd been safe in knowing that he had other people to feed from. Where was Anthony, anyway? He was a Salerno, which was one of the larger sorcerer houses, but I had no idea what that meant for potential faerie heritage. Fire faeries, probably. Most sorcerer houses had hard-ons for fire magic— one of the many reasons I'd never been scouted by a house or order as a potential recruit. I couldn't chuck a fireball, therefore I wasn't special.

Zach politely tapped my arm and then pointed to the nearest dish, some sort of roast chicken. I shrugged and helped myself. No point in letting good protein go to waste.

The others slowly followed, filling their plates and passing dishes like an awkward Thanksgiving dinner, or a last supper. The awkward silence was filled with the sounds of chewing and cutlery scraping plates. The ostentatious setting would really benefit from a string quartet, like the musicians aboard the Titanic playing music to drown by. Would anyone remember humanity when we were gone? Would anyone excavate the remains of our civilization like archeologists digging up ancient pottery shards? What happened to the inhabitants of the other worlds the demons had conquered?

Steering my mind away from those dire thoughts, I chose a new line of questioning. "What happens after we save the world? The straights are going to notice us averting the demon apocalypse. Not sure magicians can go back into hiding after that."

"We haven't really planned that far," Cat said.

I cocked an eyebrow at Zach because I was sure he'd thought ahead. He struck me as the sort who strategized for multiple contingencies. He caught my eye and shook his head with a "not here" expression. I filed it away for later.

"If we pull this off, they may not notice," Patience said. "From what I've seen of the ritual, if we time it right we can close the portals before the armies come through. It's got a solid chance of working if we have faerie magic to back us up."

And if we didn't? I wondered why the faeries had let things deteriorate this far. Sure I was familiar with delinquent parents—I still had no idea who my father was, and I was sure my mother hadn't known, either—but letting your children's world fall to a demon invasion was some A+ shitty parenting.

"Why aren't they backing us up?" I asked.

"Because they'll die," Catherine said.

"And?" I prompted.

Catherine set her fork down and her hubby glared at me for causing the interruption. "And they're not used to dying," she said. "Avoiding death is the whole reason they created Faerie in the first place. They're essentially unageing, but they're not immortal. As humanity learned how to design better slings and arrows they predictably used them on anything and everything, including the faeries and the rest of the magical creatures who live here. They didn't want to go extinct like the elves."

"Mostly extinct."

I turned to the speaker, who was seated with Patience's extended posse a few spots down from me. He wasn't part of Team Banishment, and there was something slightly off about —holy shit, those were some seriously pointed ears.

"You're an elf?" I blurted.

"Indeed. I'll exchange elven knowledge for autographed merch."

"Done!"

"The point is," Catherine interrupted, "that the faeries are terrified of dying, and they think they're safe here."

Zach reached over, took my hand and squeezed it gently.

Oh, right. I thought I was safe on my private island and that turned out to be wrong.

"They don't think we're worth saving?" I asked.

Patience snorted. "Would you consider a fruit fly worth saving? Because that's how they see us."

Anger rolled through my veins and Zach squeezed my hand again, this time to head off the magical temper tantrum tingling at my fingertips. We weren't insects. Humanity was far from perfect, but we didn't deserve extinction just because we had short lifespans. That was some speciest bullshit.

"So what do we do?" I asked.

"Eat, drink and be merry," Faust quoted dryly, "for tomorrow, we may die."

CHAPTER TEN

Ivy

For our meeting in Faerie I'd expected to arrive at a Ye Olde Conference Room as overstated as the dining hall had been, but no, instead our motley crew was transported to some sort of ancient Greek forum, the twilight scene complete with tiered stone seating, lit by torches and lanterns and encircled by honest-to-gods marble columns. I swallowed the urge to ask what faerie clan had this relic lying around their territory, but considering the political storm of arguments that was a-brewing, I kept my smart mouth shut.

At first, I was both relieved and excited to be reunited with my dogs, my ghosts (who had indeed been rescued by Anthony), and my band members. Zach eyed the boys warily, though he didn't need to. We were family, not fuck buddies, thanks to an agreement we'd made when we first formed—no inter-band romances. Too many groups had been taken down by jealousy, spouse swapping, or other affairs of the heart. More people popped into the forum who I didn't know, and that was concerning.

I found Portia attempting to convince my dogs and the

Duquesnes' dogs to all sit at the same time. Though they were all obedient dogs, there was a hell of a lot going on at once so it was understandable that their canine attention was wavering.

"Portia," I said. "What's with all the extra people?"

"Oh, the demon agents have given up on stealth and are just wholesale arresting magicians using some weird law. Or at least the American ones are, something about patriot pops? Apparently in China and Russia they don't need a reason, they can just arrest people. Rude. Anyway, faeries with close family bonds are evacuating their descendants, hence the crowd."

She returned to her obedience training tasks, and I had a minor anxiety attack. The Patriot Act. Fucking hell, was that still a thing? Were magicians with the misfortune of distant or no faerie family ties being shipped to Gitmo as we spoke? I turned to pick Zach out of the crowd—he appeared to be arguing with the Duquesnes, because of course he was.

I whistled sharply—unintentionally undermining Portia's work as all four dogs sat at once—and waved at Zach. "Hey, babe!"

True to form, my bassist Jorge answered instead. "Yes, dear?"

I flipped Jorge off. "No one likes you."

He snickered. "Aww, love you too, bitch."

I wove through the crowd to reach Zach. "Portia says the demon assholes are mass arresting magicians as suspected terrorists using the Patriot Act."

"Shit," Catherine said. "Is that still a thing?"

"I know, right?" I replied. "You'd think it would've had an expiration date. Anyway, that's why we have so many spectators. Faeries are evacuating their families."

Zach frowned. "They're not going to evacuate all of humanity, I assume?"

"Yeah, no." Catherine turned to her husband and began thumping her head against his chest as though banging her head against a wall. "Fucking hell. Now what?"

He wrapped his arms around her and held her close. "We'll figure it out."

I cleared my throat. "As much as I'm a fan of the power of positive thinking, if the demons have made a drastic change to their evil plan, we're out of time. We need to know if the faeries are going to help everyone, not just the humans they like."

"Right." Catherine sighed. "Let's get this show on the road."

The Duquesnes put on their respective Titania and Oberon hats and brought order to the chaos. Once the gathered crowd was seated, the faerie council appeared. I'd half expected a trio of faeries in business attire, but no, they were dressed in full epic fantasy cosplay. I had a new appreciation for Portia's '80s punk ensemble—at least she'd visited Earth during my lifetime. It didn't bode well for our combined fates if the faerie councils hadn't been bothered to visit our realm since the creation of theirs.

Zach tensed—like me, he was used to being on stage instead of sitting in audience. Unfortunately, our presence in Faerie remained on the thinnest of ice and we couldn't afford to shout down the people in charge solely because they were being assholes. Judging by her pinched expression, the leader of the trio, an ice faerie named Cecelia of the Silver Crescent, had been over our mortal bullshit since well before this meeting started.

"We have taken your requests to the High Council of Three," Cecelia said. Right, this was a local council, not the highest power in the realm—kind of like state senators representing our corner of Earth. "Many other councils also spoke on the behalf of humanity. However, the decision remains unchanged. We will not dissolve our home. Earth must stand on its own as it always has. We have faith in your abilities."

"Earth was created with your people as part of its magical arsenal," Lex said. "When you left our world, you took most of the magic with you. We can't stand against a demon army with depleted resources."

Cecelia's eyes narrowed. "Faerie was created because humanity hunted our kind. You have given us no guarantee of safety that the same will not happen once the demon threat has been addressed."

"Don't suppose they'll accept a pinky swear?" I muttered to Zach. He squeezed my hand in reply.

Yeah, that was a promise we couldn't make on humanity's behalf, because humanity proved again and again that we were a bunch of violent, self-destructive assholes. There was a non-zero chance that some dentist with more money than sense would want to go big game hunting for a faerie head to mount on his wall.

It was almost cynical enough for me to agree with letting humanity burn—almost, but even I wasn't that big of a bitch.

Despite the impassioned speeches made by the Duquesnes on humanity's behalf, Cecelia appeared unmoved —it was clear that these were old arguments, treading the same ground.

The faeries were going to let us all die. The certainty of our oncoming demise settled into my bones and furious magic roiled beneath my skin. If we were on Earth, the local meteorologists would be sending out storm warnings. *Dangerous weather spotted in our viewing area, take shelter now.*

Zach clasped my hand to ground me, but with our soul mate connection it created more of a feedback loop than anything calming. His inherent power fed mine, and the destructive nature of his necromantic magic coiled and danced with the rage of my inner storm.

"Enough!" Cecelia rose and folded her hands. "Mortal lives are short, and we will not risk the future of our people on the idea that our influence is the only thing that can save humanity. Your people's future is in your own hands. Only you can—"

My temper snapped and thunder cut her bullshit short. Whoops. Apparently my weather control powers worked in Faerie, too. Well, if this was the end of all things, I was going to go out with a bang, not a whimper. I rose and tugged my hand free of Zach's grasp.

The thunder rolled and crashed as I made my way to the forum floor. The Council turned their attention to me as I approached, and Catherine looked alarmed.

"Ivy, no," she whispered.

"Too late." I squared my shoulders as I faced the faerie council members. "Who are you to decide who lives and who dies?" Lightning forked through the sky above us. "You left us! Like negligent parents you abandoned magiciankind and look what happened. We're all on the edge of extinction, some more than others. What will you do when Earth falls? Sit here in your safe little bubble with those you deemed worth saving? Who do you think they'll come for next? Your world is tied to ours. Your *fate* is tied to ours. *Do something!*"

My temper reached a crescendo and lightning struck a column, shattering it into marble chunks as the spectators in the vicinity fled for cover. Sorry, not sorry.

Cecelia looked livid. "You are a guest here. Your behavior is unacceptable."

"You know what's unacceptable? Genocide." My hands balled into fists. "Every moment we waste here is another magician life ended on Earth, and we didn't have an abundant population to start with."

"She's right," Catherine said. I blinked in surprise—I'd expected her to continue politicking. "We can't keep dancing around the subject. Will you help us defend Earth, yes or no?"

"No."

My stomach dropped—holy fucking shit, they really were abandoning us.

Cecelia continued, "The clans will continue to accept any of their descendants who wish to take refuge here, but we will not participate in your war. That is our final word on this subject. This meeting is adjourned."

And just like that, the council vanished and left us to our fate.

~

Zach

I tensed, expecting to be evicted from Faerie that moment, but when nothing happened I hurried down the marble steps to join Ivy.

"Are you crazy?" I asked her. She quirked an unimpressed green eyebrow.

"Of all the things I've lost, I miss my mind the most," she deadpanned. Catherine snorted, but her husband was not amused.

"What *are* you?" Duquesne asked.

"Taken," I replied before Ivy could answer. "I suggest that the present members of the pan-magician adjourn to decide our next steps."

Ivy patted his shoulder. "That's a very polite way to say let's blow this popsicle stand."

"We're having popsicles now?" Portia appeared beside Catherine, who then turned to address her cousin.

"Yes. We're going back to Castle Silverleaf and we're all having popsicles. Except the dogs, they'd eat the sticks."

"That's true," Ivy said.

For the first—and probably last—time, Alexander Duquesne and I locked eyes and shared the same look of exasperation.

"Can we come, too?" Ivy's band member, Paz, asked. "We want to help cancel the apocalypse."

Catherine nodded. "Okay. Everyone gather your extended people and we'll leave for Castle Silverleaf in five minutes."

I turned and picked Anthony out of the crowd and then beckoned him to join us. I spotted a few additional employees, most importantly my healer, Amelia, and motioned to them as well. I'd give them the option of fighting—or whatever action we decided to take—or staying safe. Not all my people were capable of combat.

When our larger group assembled, we were ported to an empty ballroom in Castle Silverleaf.

"Ooh, faerie instruments," Wolfgang said. Ivy caught him by the collar of his shirt before he could escape.

"No. Focus, Wolfie."

Paz raised his hand like a grade school student. "Umm, please tell me there's a magical Death Star waiting in the wings to nuke the demons from orbit."

Ivy shot me an "I told you so" glance and I had a renewed appreciation of her ability to survive long bus rides with her bandmates.

Catherine tapped her chin. "We really should have thought of that earlier."

Duquesne whistled for order. "We need to move fast. Serious suggestions only."

Patience snorted behind me and muttered, "That'd be a first."

"Okay," Ivy said. "We need to seal the doors to the hell realms all on our lonesome before the demons start mass murdering humanity." She paused and peered at the Titania and Oberon. "Is there a group chat for Titanias and Oberons? A Slack channel?"

"Yeah, pretty much," Catherine agreed. "Just less simple and more archaic. We have the leaders of several different regions working on the problem, too."

"They've also come up with snake eyes on the subject so far," Patience said. "And there are almost no summoners left who I've been able to reach. They're either dead or in hiding."

"Are there more soul mates?"

The group turned toward Anne Williams in surprise—the seer was typically silent during these meetings. She cleared her throat and continued. "Have the other Titanias seen an increase in their local soul mate population?" She waved a hand at the crowd. "All these matches can't be a local thing. They started showing up about the same time as the hunters appeared."

"Not sure. We'll ask," Catherine said.

"Well, we know it's not a local phenomenon." Nati nodded to her soul mate, Cris—they were both part of Patience and Faust's banishing team. "We met in Spain."

"Soul mates?" Jorge whispered to Ivy.

She grinned and leaned up to kiss my cheek. "Yup! I won the jackpot."

Paz pouted. "Not fair. I want a sexy billionaire soul mate, too."

"It makes sense." Portia tilted her head. "Magic like this should be distributed evenly through the weave, not concentrated in one place."

My least favorite cousin, Simon St. Jerome, made a choking sound. "The weave is real? It's not magical theory?"

Portia scoffed and rolled her eyes. "Of course it's real. Everyone knows that."

I covered my surprised laugh with a cough as the assembled librarians facepalmed in unison.

Catherine sighed. "I don't think any of us are familiar with that term, cousin."

Portia frowned, appearing deep in thought, and then snapped her fingers. "Oh! Popsicles! I forgot."

An assortment of the frozen treats in question appeared on a buffet table. Ivy patted my shoulder and sauntered over to select one for herself.

Catherine stared at the ballroom ceiling, likely gathering the last remaining shreds of her calm judging by her expression—usually said expression was directed toward me in our pan-magician meetings.

Simon cleared his throat. "Lady Silverleaf, if you would please be so kind as to explain what the weave is to those who haven't heard of it?"

The faerie conjured a chair to perch on. "It's like it sounds. The legend is that when the higher powers created the worlds, they wove everything on a divine loom. That's why all the worlds are connected. The doors aren't really doors, they're threads. And there are different layers. Like, magic has its own layer of the weave."

"Oh," Anne said. "That's why I see the connections between soul mates as threads."

"And the weave between them grows stronger over time," Emily Black continued. "The tighter the weave—"

"—the more powerful the magicians are together," Catherine finished. "Holy shit. We could really do this. We just need to snip the threads connecting our world to the hell dimensions."

"Before the demons wipe out magic," Portia added. The room seemed to hold its collective breath.

"Pardon?" I asked.

Portia shrugged. "When we created Faerie, we took a lot of Earth's magic with us—and its magical creatures, like dragons—so you're already at a disadvantage. It's probably why the magician population is so small. Less magic, less magic users to wield it."

"And the less magic users there are..." Catherine prompted.

"The weaker the magic weave. No magic, no weave. No weave, no barriers keeping the bad things out."

"The demons aren't just taking out the magicians to make sure no one can banish them," Patience said. "They're trying to shred Earth's defenses."

When we created Faerie, we took a lot of Earth's magic with us.

I turned to Faust and caught his eye—or at least I thought I did, it was always hard to tell with his dark glasses. He inclined his head in a slight nod to acknowledge me, but then he shook his head. *Not here.*

Faust had been campaigning for the dissolution of Faerie for years, and Helen for longer than that. The argument was that dissolving the realm would allow the faeries to regain their lost fertility—a theory that seemed correct considering that Patience was carrying his child. A magical mishap had transformed her from a mortal summoner into a full-blooded faerie.

Unmaking Faerie would give us a fighting chance. And the faeries refused to help.

Ivy nudged me with her elbow and I focused my attention on my soul mate. Her brow rose as she sucked on her popsicle, and that lovely image was a distraction I did not need at the moment. Thankfully Paz took pity on me and relieved his band member of her frozen treat.

"Problem?" Ivy asked.

"Not yet."

Catherine cleared her throat. "Okay, Lex and I are going to step out for a bit to coordinate the global Care Bear stare with our counterparts. Class dismissed. Everyone rest up."

Portia, Catherine and Duquesne were ported from the room, and I gestured toward Faust and Simon.

"Family meeting time."

CHAPTER ELEVEN

Ivy

The "family" in question for attendance of the family meeting consisted of me and Zach, Faust and Patience, and Anne the psychic and her vampire librarian honey, Simon. Apparently Patience and Faust bunked with Simon at his lair—or library, rather—though that didn't mean much to a couple who could teleport. And, fun fact, Faust was Zach's uncle and Simon's father.

Judging by the sour expressions on everyone's faces, I suspected that this meeting was not called for family bonding time. I decided to break the awkward ice. "It's not going to work, is it?"

"It might work," Faust said. "Anything is possible."

Patience patted his shoulder. "Motivational speaking is not your strong suit, dear."

I cleared my throat. "You don't think Earth has enough magical fuel left to power the Care Bear stare."

"Can we please not call it that?" Zach asked.

"No problem, Grumpy Bear." I squeezed his hand and he sighed.

"I believe my original plan is most likely to succeed," Faust said.

"And, for what it's worth, I agree with him." Anne pinched the bridge of her nose. "But the future is hard to see."

"Yeah, I learned that from Yoda." I flopped into a richly upholstered loveseat and dragged my soul mate to sit beside me. The father, the son, and the billionaire nephew all looked confused by the fast-flying pop culture references. "Anyway, the point is, acquiring faerie help was our best bet at survival and they shut that option down. So why are we here? Planning a heist before the world ends?"

Faust shook his head. "Not a heist. Simply a contingency plan."

"Like what?" I asked. "We start a social media challenge to clap for Tinkerbell and trick the world into believing in faeries again? Poison Apples has a huge fanbase, we can make it happen."

"I like your enthusiasm," Patience said. "But belief won't do it. Magic didn't fade in our world because people stopped believing. It faded because people started burning magicians at the stake. And drowning them. And—"

"Are we *sure* that straights can't banish demons?" I asked. "I feel like a grenade pretty much says 'go to hell' with no magic involved."

"Banishing only delays the inevitable at this point." Zach squared his shoulders and turned to Faust. "You might as well tell them. This was your plan."

"No, this was Helen's plan," Faust replied. "I was attempting to find a more diplomatic solution."

"We have an evil backup plan?" I asked.

"It's not evil, per se," Faust scoffed.

Patience shrugged. "Babe, you do dress like you're about to ruin date night for a superhero."

Faust quirked an eyebrow. "Pot, kettle?"

"Excuse you, I make this look good." Patience fluttered her flaming wings for emphasis. "Plus, I was never on the side of the good guys. I'm the morally gray character who switches sides when it serves her purpose. And not dying serves my purpose right about now."

Zach rolled his eyes and I elbowed him. "Don't laugh, Lex Luthor. We're the bad guys in this scenario? I didn't pack my leather catsuit."

Zach's brow rose. "I will happily buy you all the leather catsuits you want."

I grinned and Patience cracked her knuckles. "I can absolutely make it rain leather catsuits up in here—"

Simon cleared his throat, presumably because he hated fun, and raised his voice. "What is Helen's plan?"

"In the most basic terms, to pop Faerie like a balloon."

"You know how to accomplish that?" Simon asked Faust.

"No, but Helen does. She's been obsessing about it since our clan was cast out. Well, a version of it, at any rate." Faust removed his glasses and pinched the bridge of his nose. "Unmaking Faerie was—is—our best bet for regaining faerie fertility, and that was Helen's focus."

"You knocked up your soul mate," I said.

Patience patted his shoulder. "Sure did, but I wasn't born a faerie. I used to be a summoner, so I'm a special case. The bottom line is that unmaking Faerie will return fertility to the faeries and an unknown quantity of magic to Earth, which will have all sorts of fun consequences we can't predict."

Simon frowned. "That does not endear me to this plan."

"Yeah, I don't think anyone in here is excited about that option," I said. "I mean, yes, we'd all like to cancel the apocalypse and live to fight another day, but that option puts all magicians and magical beings back on the endangered species lists. You know the same assholes who hunt elephants for trophies are going to hunt unicorns, and—"

"I know," Anne said softly. "I've seen all the terrible options. It boils down to the trolley problem."

Patience cocked her head. "The what now?"

I groaned and cursed, and Anne smiled. "I see you're familiar."

"Yeah, Jorge likes to torture us with ethics thought puzzles to get back at Paz for all his fanboy shit. There are different variations, but the basic one is this." I raised my hands, palms up, like I was balancing a scale. "A trolley's traveling down its tracks and its brakes have failed. You're a bystander standing next to a switch. If you do nothing, the trolley will flatten five people on the main track. If you flip the switch, you flatten one poor bastard. How do you choose who lives and who dies?"

"Right," Anne said. "Say humanity's the five people on the main track. If we do nothing, they're goners. If we flip the switch, we save humanity, but who gets flattened instead? Faeries? Magicians? And what happens down the line? Flipping the switch doesn't fix the brake problem. Will more people get killed?"

"I have an all-new appreciation for how much it must suck to be a seer," I said.

Anne snorted. "Thanks. Want to trade?"

"Pretty sure you don't want my brand of magical angst, either."

I shrank back as everyone's attention focused on me. Zach caught my hand and held it, and he sat up straighter as though daring anyone to interrogate me.

I cleared my throat. "Okay, all other moral decisions are moot at the moment, because we're going with Plan A."

"And when that fails?" Faust asked.

Zach squeezed my hand. "Then things get bloody."

"Business as usual, then," Faust said. "We'll check in with the Titania."

Faust and Patience vanished, leaving us with Simon and Anne, and I turned to her. "You know something."

She squirmed and edged closer to her soul mate. "That's very vague."

"You know something about us and how this ends." I gestured between me and Zach.

"I've seen several possible futures. That's how my magic works."

"Anne, please," Zach said. I blinked, surprised by his gentle tone.

She sighed, and then leaned into Simon as he wrapped his arms around her—she seemed to find strength in his embrace, which was probably par for the soul mate course. Stronger together than apart and all that jazz. I glanced down at our joined hands and wondered what Zach and I were capable of doing together. Popping Faerie like a balloon? My inner meteorological disaster enthusiast was all about that idea—a storm to end all storms. My magic crackled at the possibility.

"We go out with a bang?" I asked. "Die a hero, or live long enough to become the villain?"

"I already am the villain," Zach muttered. I raised our entwined hands and kissed his knuckles.

"Not to me."

"You're the bystander," Anne informed us. "And whatever choice you make, it's going to be bloody and final."

"And on that note, meeting adjourned," I declared.

Zach

Ivy paced the perimeter of our guest room, a ball of anxious, frenetic energy, until I stood in her path and let her crash into me. I wrapped my arms around her and brushed a kiss against her hair.

"It's going to be okay," I murmured.

"Nothing about any of this is okay." She tilted her head to meet my eyes. "It's the fucking apocalypse and apparently we have some special be-all, end-all decision to make."

"And we'll make it together."

"What if it's the wrong decision?"

My lips twisted with a wry smile. "I think we're both used to making the wrong decision."

"For ourselves, yeah." Ivy scowled. "This is far-reaching-consequences shit. The worst thing that normally happens when I really fuck up is that we have to refund concert tick-ets. You can't refund failing to save the world."

"Then we'll save it."

Her eyes narrowed. "You're being strangely composed about all this."

"I'd say it was based on the power of positive thinking, but it's not. I know I'm not a hero, but I'm going to do my best. That's all we can do."

Ivy grumbled and thumped her forehead against my chest. "How much time do we have before we leave for the spell?"

"About three hours, give or take."

"Hmm. I guess that'll do."

"Do?" I quirked an eyebrow and Ivy smirked up at me.

"For 'Last Night on Earth' sex. It's an important part of preparing for the final battle."

I laughed as she waggled her eyebrows. "Let me guess, this is the sort of discussion you have while trapped on a bus with your band mates."

"You, sir, are correct. In fact I can almost guarantee that

Paz has called in Wolfie's promise that they'd exchange blowjobs if the world was about to end."

I snorted and shook my head as I tried to scrub that image out of my mind. Instead I framed her face with my hands—my beautiful, brilliant, brave soul mate. She'd already endured so much, it wasn't fair to ask this of her but we had no choice. I leaned in and kissed her long and slow, savoring the moment. I wanted a lifetime with Ivy, but now we might only have a handful of hours left.

"I'm sorry," I said.

"For?"

"All the things I should have done to keep us together six years ago. For being so afraid of turning out like my parents that I avoided anything that looked remotely like a relationship."

"Hey." Ivy poked my chest. "No point in playing the 'what-if' game, especially when we've only got three hours. Get naked and get in bed."

"Yes, ma'am."

"**T**his is a terrible idea."

Zach nodded his agreement to my muttered comment as we gathered around a giant mirrored jellybean in Millennium Park. The argument had been made —loudly and repeatedly by magicians who knew far more about ritual magic than I did—in favor of using the Chicago landmark for the spell that would shut the doors to the hell realms. Mirrors were good for portal magic, and because we were casting a big-ass portal spell it made sense to utilize a big-ass mirror. Or an anti-portal spell, I supposed. Either way, terrible idea.

The surviving members of the pan-magician council gathered with Team Soul Mates and formed a ring around the Bean, freezing our collective asses off as midnight approached, because magicians who knew more about ritual magic than I did insisted that the time of day was essential to casting the spell. Whatever. The important part was that our faeries had created some sort of invisibility glamour to shield us from prying eyes while we worked our magic.

Being outside of Faerie made me uneasy. Faerie was a safe space where the hunters couldn't arrest me and Zach for whatever bullshit reason they'd concocted to sell to the media. Would the demons know we'd returned? Did they have some sort of magical tracking spell queued to us? It would explain how they'd known to lie in wait in the parking garage at the end of Zach's escape tunnel.

"All right, everyone ready?" Catherine asked. Her forced cheer grated on my nerves as my good sense continued to silently chant a list of all the ways that this could go wrong.

I was fully aware that doubt wasn't helpful to spellcasting because much of magic depended on the will to make it happen, but I couldn't help it. I was a philanthropist, and my idea of saving the world revolved around writing checks, not chanting a ritual in bastardized Latin at a tourist attraction.

I took Zach's hand and held on for dear life—handholding was a ritual requirement of the soul mates in attendance. I chalked it up to the weave thing that Portia had described. What would our magic look like when it was woven together? Combining my tempest magic with Zach's bizarre brand of faerie blood, alchemy and necromancy probably resembled a new age goth nightmare.

The Titania and Oberon began the spell, initiating the call and response. The Bean was massive and its bulk blocked my view of portions of the group. Simon and Anne were to our right, with Patience and Faust to their right. To our left stood Nati and Cris, and Nati appeared as nervous as I felt, which did not bode well for our success rate.

The chant swelled and my inner musician shoved the chant of doubt aside and happily glommed onto the spell's rhythm. The soothing rise and fall reminded me of the gentle swell of calm waves lapping against a beach. My magic reached out and connected with the massive bulk of Lake Michigan and the spell swelled with a power surge.

The gleaming surface of the Bean clouded as it was covered with dozens—maybe hundreds—of images of portals. Zach tightened his grip on my hand as though attempting to prevent me from touching the obvious danger, and I decided his caution was fair. After all, I did have a well-known history of making poor life choices, but even my self-destructive curiosity wasn't strong enough to justify touching a portal to a hell dimension.

They were fascinating to look at, though. I wasn't a summoner, but I knew enough demon lore to know that there wasn't one single hell. After all, evil took many forms, and every society had its own recipe for ultimate evil. Plus, these weren't areas of the afterlife. We weren't closing the gates to Tartarus or Purgatory, if those places even existed. No, judging by the images drifting across the surface of the Bean, these were worlds with smothering shadows, devouring flames, killing frost, and gods only knew what else.

The spell shifted to phase two—now that we'd conjured an image of the portals, we planned to cut earth's connection to them. The chant changed, and I gasped and swayed as our ritual synched with the others being performed around the globe by other groups of Titanias, Oberons and soul mates. We were connected by a weave that spanned oceans, rivers, streams... Water held the power to purify, to wash away the poisonous grime of the hell realms. We weren't alone. We could do this.

Something tugged at the edge of my thoughts—*poison*. If we really wanted to kill these connections, then we shouldn't just cut them, we should cauterize them. The thought slipped away as the spell demanded my attention. A sharp inhale from my left clued me in that something was happening, and I gaped as a group of gray portals vanished. One hell down, several more to go.

The process repeated once, twice, but then I frowned as the mirror surface of the Bean clouded and obscured the remaining portals. A slight hiss underlaid the chant and I searched for the source of the sound. *Steam.* A blast of heat shoved the circle and hissing wisps of steam curled across the mirror surface as several fiery portals swelled in size. Panicked, I pulled on the power of the lake and tried to drown them, and a few smaller images winked out. The troublesome flaming portals were unaffected and continued to expand.

"Patience," I said.

"Yeah, I see it," the faerie answered. "Incoming!"

The portals exploded and shattered the surface of the Bean, and the concussive wave scattered our group like leaves on the wind. I landed on my back and the impact knocked the breath from my lungs, and Zach threw himself over me to shield from flaming chunks of modern art that sprayed in every direction. I rolled us aside to avoid being trampled by invading demons pouring from the portals—the creatures looked nothing like the ones that had shown up at my haunted mansion. Instead of oily shadows the demons were tall, spindly four-legged creatures made of flames, fangs and claws.

Great. Now we were responsible for causing the second Chicago Fire. Our PR people were going to *love* that.

Zach scrambled to his feet and hauled me up with him. "Are you all right?"

"Fine. You?"

He nodded as we caught the attention of the nearest fire demons and they rounded on us. I planted my feet, thrust my hands forward and unleashed a torrent of water worthy of a high-pressure fire hose. The demons were doused and presumably banished, but with an open portal just a few feet away that did a fat lot of good. Zach grabbed my arm and we retreated to stand with Patience, Faust and the rest of their extended family and banishing team.

"This is gonna be livestreaming momentarily, isn't it?" I asked.

"Yup," Patience said. "The glamour is definitely trashed."

I drenched a new wave of flaming fucks. "New plan?"

Zach cursed and I turned and followed his line of sight—portals were opening throughout the park and along the neighboring Michigan Avenue.

"I think they moved up the invasion timetable," Zach said.

Well, shit.

~

Zach

Fear squeezed my chest as I stood paralyzed by the sight of the demon tide flooding downtown Chicago. The previous midnight calm was filled with a cacophony of inhuman snarls, shrieks and growls combined with sirens, car horns and screams.

We failed. Judging by the portals that had vanished from the Bean, the spell had closed off three, possibly four of the realms we'd targeted. On one hand, every bit helped, but on the other...our world was still well and truly fucked.

"Cover me." Ivy shucked her singed winter coat, and the air around her crackled with power as though she radiated a vicious amount of static electricity. Thunder rumbled as clouds formed and covered the night sky, and the storm startled me out of my moment of panic. We'd lost the battle but not the war.

I turned to Faust. "We need to prep an evac."

Faust lobbed a fireball toward a group of squat shadow demons. "I don't know if our invitation to Faerie still stands."

"My guess is no." Anne crouched and fired a handgun—seers had no offensive magic—into the same group. "Think we could get an Uber?"

"I have vehicles at the tower if we can make it there." I grabbed a trash can and hurled it at a hellhound who showed too much interest in our group. "It's about a mile from here."

"What about the others?" Nati lobbed a potion grenade that banished a group of fire demons on impact. "I don't see them."

My fists clenched as I realized that I couldn't see or hear the rest of the people who had gathered to cast our spell. "Patience? Faust? Aerial view?"

"No," Ivy said. "Stay down. I don't want to accidentally hit you."

"With what?" Patience asked.

As though in answer, lightning streaked from the sky and struck several spots around us, and demons screamed and vanished under the assault.

"Holy shit!" Patience belatedly ducked and covered, and I silently echoed the sentiment.

"Don't worry about the others," Faust said. "Their invitations to retreat to Faerie are ensured."

I grimaced and nodded. The Duquesnes and the were-tigers all had faerie relatives to look after them.

"Michael and Emily don't share those invitations," Simon said.

I cursed. I had no love for Mr. and Mrs. Black, but they were precious to Anne, and I intended to stay in the seer's good graces. Plus I supposed that I should be considerate to Simon since he was my family, and he considered them his family.

"Fine," I said. "We need to shift left to look for them."

"We need to get away from the lake shore," Ivy said. "There's a wave incoming."

"What? Like a tsunami? How?" Patience asked.

Thunder cracked and a cold, driving rain suddenly poured from the conjured storm. Angry howls and clouds of steam rose from the clumps of fire demons.

"Less talk, more running," Ivy said.

Patience shrugged. "Right. Cris, Nati, we're clearing a path to check for survivors."

"Here." Cris pressed a pair of spell grenades into my hands. "I assume you know how these work."

"In theory. My alchemical experience was more party and less combat."

"And all fabulous," Ivy added. She thrust her hands forward and conjured a blast of water. Cris, Nati and I added our grenades to the area and then we moved as a group.

The wide plaza surrounding the sculpture was littered with debris and empty of places to take shelter. Simon shouted for Michael and Emily as we moved, and I focused on defending my soul mate. Ivy stumbled as though drunk, her focus split between moving and maintaining the storm. I scooped her up in a princess carry and she yelped indignantly.

"Focus on the storm," I said. "There's not a lot I can do, too many fire creatures."

"Ugh. Fine. We'll argue later." Ivy closed her eyes and lightning struck several scaled, reptilian demons clustered where Michael and Emily Black and Marie Duquesne and Dr. Dannaher had been standing during the ritual. Marie was a guardian, so the odds were good that she and her soul mate had been evacuated.

"Down here!"

Simon darted toward Michael's voice. He vaulted over a stone fence that ringed the plaza and disappeared from view. I peered down into the empty courtyard of the restaurant below the Bean.

"Go, we're right behind you," Patience said. Faust was already floating down with Anne, Nati and Cris held in a levitation spell. I hugged Ivy closer and leaped. The landing was slightly slippery and I mentally kicked myself for not wearing boots.

Michael and Emily Black had taken shelter in the entryway for the closed restaurant. I set Ivy on her feet and she leaned against me.

"We have to move," she said.

"How big of a wave are we talking?" I asked.

"Don't know. Never tried it before." Ivy shrugged. "Big enough to wipe out any fire portals and demons along the lake shore."

"Not quite disaster movie proportions," Patience said. "How the fuck are you managing that?"

"It appears that Ivy is a tempest," Faust said. "I rather thought they were extinct. Our little family is quite extraordinary."

"Where are the others?" Michael asked.

"We intended to ask you that," Simon said.

Michael shook his head. "We lost sight of them after the explosion. We were forced to take shelter."

The rain turned to sleet and then hail, and hailstones the size of pennies bounced on the concrete like bizarre popcorn kernels.

"We need to run," Ivy said.

"Simon and I will take point," Faust said. "Patience and Zachary will cover our rear. Everyone else look after each other."

We ran.

I hadn't given much thought to what the demon invasion would look like. I'd battled demons, hunters and other necromancers over the past several months, but those confrontations paled in comparison to the onslaught as the demons poured from the portals and streamed into the city. The demons were done hiding behind human masks, finished waiting on the countdown to enacting their master plan. They were here to wipe out humanity.

Chicago is a city of roughly three million people, if you include the surrounding suburbs, and it's never truly quiet. Midnight was hardly late enough for the streets to be empty, and people were running or trapped in their cars. I looked back as someone in our group hesitated, and I spotted Nati as she paused on the sidewalk, her expression distraught. As part of Patience's banishing team, Nati was doubtless used to saving people.

"Keep moving," I shouted. "You can't help them."

"We have to do something," Nati said.

"We can't help them if we die here," I said. "Go!"

It felt like the longest mile of my life. As a master necromancer I could have enhanced my speed and crossed the distance in moments, but we had too many people in our group who weren't blessed with supernatural speed—my soul mate among them. Our group dodged wrecked cars and flaming debris, and judging by the chaos the weather created I assumed that Ivy had lost control of her storm. A tornado siren began howling as we passed the halfway point—had the storm spawned a tornado, or had some enterprising city employee decided to use it as a makeshift tsunami warning?

I glanced back, and my enhanced night vision spotted the wall of water framed between the canyon walls created by the buildings lining the street.

"We're out of time!" I grabbed Ivy, threw her over my shoulder and sprinted. I trusted that the others capable of enhanced speed would follow suit.

Ivy shouted an impressive string of curses as I zoomed toward my tower. The wards held and the river of demons parted around the edges of the spell, and I stopped at the building's entrance and set my soul mate down. I turned and waited for the others. Faust and Patience arrived first carrying Cris and Nati, followed by Simon carrying Anne and finally Michael and Emily.

A group of paparazzi and nightcrawler camera crews huddled near the entrance, likely bewildered by why the demons weren't coming closer.

Ivy pointed at the humans. "We need them. You get the door."

I grimaced—she was right, the media would be useful in warning the masses, but that didn't mean I had to like it. I input my access code and unlocked the entrance, and then shepherded everyone into the tower's foyer.

"Do you have a comment?" One of the paps thrust a camera toward me and I fixed it with a dry expression.

"We need to get higher." I quickly estimated the size of our larger group and turned to Faust. "Penthouse. Two cars."

Faust nodded and we herded everyone to the elevators. Faust and I were the only ones with access to the penthouse, so we each took one group. The building shuddered and the lights flickered during our ascent, but thankfully the power remained on and everyone reached our destination intact. Ivy and I hustled to the windows and looked down as the massive wave surrounded the base of the tower and continued past to meet the nearby fork of the Chicago River.

"What the fuck was that?" A photographer stood beside me and gaped at the sight.

"That bought us time," I said. "It's the end of world, and we need your help."

I'd experimented with creating mild waves while living in my haunted mansion, mainly as a tool to swamp the boats of enterprising reporters who wanted to invade my island of solitude—the reporters were unharmed, but I succeeded in drowning their expensive equipment. As such, I was unprepared for the power of the wave I'd unleashed on Chicago, but at least it had the desired effect of wiping out the portals in its path. I'd worry about the lives lost and property damage incurred if we lived through this.

Zach and I gave a brief statement to our rescued media representatives about what was going on and how to deal with it, hoping that the message would reach the masses and do some good. Team Banishment was glued to the penthouse's giant TV, watching the end times play out around the world live in high def. Judging by the reporting, things did not bode well for mankind. Considering how quickly things seemed to be falling apart—power grids shutting down, communication channels cutting off—the demons had used their military and federal agent personas for more than hunting magicians.

Clever bastards had figured out all the fastest ways to cripple our technology.

I grabbed Zach's arm, hauled him into the bedroom and locked the door behind us.

"We need Helen's plan," I said.

"I know." Zach sighed and tugged a hand through his hair. "Mother?"

Helen appeared in the room, singed, bleeding and scowling. "Well. That was bracing."

"Are you okay?" I asked. This was the first time I'd seen her not appear impeccably put together.

She waved a dismissive hand. "I'm well enough. The Shadow Realm is quite congested at the moment. Thankfully I'm not the easy target that the demons seem to think I am." Helen bared her teeth in a bloody grin, and then she studied us both with a tilted head. "My darlings, are you both well?"

"We're fine," Zach assured her. "We lost contact with the rest of the council when the ritual was interrupted."

Helen shrugged. "Our family survived, that's what matters."

I opened my mouth to argue but decided to save the oxygen—there was no point in arguing that point with the unstable faerie. "What do we need to do to unmake Faerie?"

"It's surprising simple, considering the current circumstances." Helen peered out the windows at the city below. "Oh my. Ivy, darling, did you conjure this storm? It's impressive."

"Conjure, yes. I've lost control of it, though." And damn, it was distracting. The effects of the storm raged beneath my skin like someone replaced my blood with concentrated caffeine. Could I regain control of it? Probably, but the effort would absolutely kick my magic's ass. I needed sleep and calories, and we didn't have time for one and somehow I doubted that Zach had energy bars squirreled away in his penthouse kitchen for the other.

"Hmm. That may make travel difficult." Helen frowned. "We can't chance moving you through the Shadow Realm, it's much too risky. I assume the mortal roads will also be a challenge."

"A helicopter is probably also a no considering the storm," I said.

"Where are we traveling to?" Zach asked.

"You need a place of power to amplify the spell," Helen said.

I shrugged, and Zach appeared equally confused.

"Let's ask the librarians," I said.

Zach nodded and then reached out to gently touch Helen's shoulder. "Mother, Ivy and I need all of our companions alive. Including Mr. and Mrs. Black."

Helen scowled. "I don't know why you need that particular pair alive, but we hardly have time to act on personal grudges. After, however—"

"Mother, no. They are dear to Faust's son."

Helen huffed and folded her arms, and I figured that was as good as we were going to get.

"One place of power, coming up." I turned and walked away to find our librarians.

Nati apparently had media experience—before joining Team Banishment, she worked as a researcher for a cable history channel—and was utilizing our rescued reporters to get the word out to the masses about the best strategies for surviving the demon apocalypse. I left her alone and approached Simon and Michael.

"We need a local place of power," I announced.

Both men asked, "Why?" in unison. Anne looked up from her spot on the couch.

"There's one on our property," she said.

Simon waved dismissively. "That's a witch's circle."

"Which is a place of power," Anne countered.

I turned toward the doorway to the bedroom where Helen waited, studying the scene with a worrisome expression. Damn it, we did not have time for crazy faerie mama drama.

"Will that work?" I asked her.

"We'll make do." Helen shrugged. "You'll likely need the aid of the rest of your soul mate companions. Once the ritual begins it will attract the attention of both demons and faeries."

"We don't know where they are," Simon said stiffly. He had shifted subtly to put himself between Helen and Michael.

"Has anyone tried calling them?" I asked.

"Portia isn't answering," Simon said.

"I mean with a cell phone. The networks are still up, right?" I turned to Nati and her news team, and she nodded with a thumbs-up. I quirked an eyebrow at Zach. "I know you have Catherine's contact info."

Simon muttered, "Brian."

"On it." Michael pulled a phone from the inner pocket of his suit jacket to call Dr. Dannaher, Marie Duquesne's soul mate. While I felt that much of our group was overdressed for the end of the world, the undead librarians did look distinguished.

"Where is your property?" I asked Simon.

"LaGrange." His brow furrowed. "It's about fifteen miles away, but I doubt that the roads will be clear."

"That's a definite no," Nati said. "We're getting reports of accidents pretty much everywhere. Law enforcement is asking people to shelter in place."

"Not the worst idea." I returned to Helen's side before she got any ideas. "Okay, what else?"

"You'll need to recite this spell." A piece of cream-colored stationary appeared, topped with the words *From the Desk of Helen Harrison*. I grimaced at the flowery penmanship that filled the page—great, more Latin. "You are the conduit for the spell. Zachary will ground you—he's your connection to this world. If you lose control of this spell, well..." Helen glanced out the windows at the storm raging around the tower. "It's imperative that you work together."

"Why me? Why us?"

Helen smiled. "My dear, I have it on good authority that your words are poison."

I snorted. "Right. In that case, I need some blank sheet music, a guitar and an amp. You figure out the transportation. I'll make the spell work."

Zach

"Do you have a comment, Mr. Harrison?"

After seeing Ivy settled into the bedroom to compose music to save the world with I returned to the penthouse's living room to stare at the storm raging around us. The others had given me space to brood, but an intrepid paparazzo had inched close with his camera. He was young, likely a novice who'd been looking to score big with footage of Ivy and myself.

"Shouldn't you be coordinating with the others?" I asked.

He shrugged. "I'm livestreaming."

"What would you like me to comment on?"

"Did you know this was coming?"

"The apocalypse?" I asked, and he nodded. "I had hoped climate change would get us first. It may still, if we live through this."

"Do you have anything to say to my viewers? Famous last words?"

I laughed—I tried to imagine any words of wisdom that I could come up with echoing through the halls of history. I thought of Catherine and Patience, who both pulled no punches when sharing their opinions of me. A wry smile tugged at my lips as I turned toward the camera.

"I've often been reminded recently that I'm 'famous for being famous' and not for contributing anything of worth to society." I scrubbed my face with my hands. "All I can say is that we need to do better. Humanity has a long history of destroying things we don't understand. That's how we got here. Humans didn't understand magic, so they hunted it. No one paused to consider what the consequences of that might be, and now here we are."

I gestured at the view of the city.

"But you have a plan, right?" he asked. "To save us?"

"We're working on it."

Nati rescued me before the man could ask additional questions, and she dragged him back to the group of journalists to broadcast something or other. I located Faust clustered with the rest of Team Banishment, discussing battle plans for defending the witch's circle on Simon's property. Faust peeled off from the group at my approach.

"Something wrong?" he asked.

"At this point, it would be more notable if something went right. How are the plans working out?"

Faust grimaced and nodded. "We'll do our best. It helps that it's Simon's land. He has a connection to it, and we have a connection to him."

A petty part of me wanted to reject the idea of any connection to my least favorite cousin, but that wouldn't help our situation.

Faust studied me with a pensive expression. "If this works, the faeries won't thank us for it. We might not live to enjoy our victory."

"I know. One problem at a time." I squeezed his shoulder, and then I squeaked in undignified surprise when he pulled me into a tight hug.

"I'm proud of you, Zachary," he said. "Never doubt that."

I blinked, stunned. I couldn't remember the last time he'd hugged me, but I assumed that he'd stopped when I was twelve or thirteen and I decided that I was "too old" for such things. In retrospect, that was a bullshit reason, and considering that Faust had been the one constant in my life who always supported me I silently vowed to do better at showing my appreciation for him.

"I—thank you."

"Aww, can I get in on the hug fest?" Patience asked.

"No," I said in reflex. She wrinkled her nose.

"Not you, you have vampire cooties." She embraced Faust and he shot me an apologetic look. I huffed a dry laugh and decided to retreat to my bedroom to sit with Ivy while she worked.

I quietly let myself into the room. Ivy sat in an armchair with an acoustic guitar, and papers were scattered atop the nightstand she'd dragged over to create a makeshift workspace. She hummed and tapped her foot as she worked on the spell, pausing to jot down the occasional note. Her hair was singed in spots from the Bean's explosion—I cringed at the potential bill for that destruction—and soot smudged her face.

She was beautiful and determined, and I didn't deserve her.

"Sit," she ordered.

For a moment I looked around for her dogs, who were back at Castle Silverleaf with the Duquesnes' pets. Would they be safe if we unmade Faerie? No one knew the specifics of what would happen, though Helen seemed certain that the structures would return to their original locations. Considering how much the landscape had changed over the millennia since Faerie was formed, some voids were about to be surprised with new magical neighbors.

Ivy pointed to the spot on the floor beside her chair and I cocked an eyebrow.

"I beg your pardon?"

"Sit here," she said. "And be quiet. The soul mate connection will help ground me as long as you don't distract me."

With nothing else to do, I shrugged and obeyed. I closed my eyes and slipped into an almost meditative state as she worked. My mind drifted, wondering what a world where faeries, magicians and the voids lived together would look like? Faust had told me stories of what it had been like the first time—magic wasn't all-powerful, and enough unwashed peasants with torches and pitchforks could ruin even the most powerful magic user's day. I'd like to think that modern humans were more advanced, more tolerant, but—

Ivy flicked my head. "Knock it off, you're harshing my mellow."

I flinched away from her and scowled. "You could sense that?"

"Yes. You're oozing negativity. Positive vibes only or I'll kick you out and you can spend some quality time with mommy dearest."

I shuddered—maybe I should be riding herd on Helen.

Powers only knew what she could be telling our tiny group of media refugees.

"How can you keep a positive outlook about all this?" I asked.

"Practice." She smiled dryly. "I've been through some truly awful shit. The only way to keep moving forward is to hang on to the hope that things will be better. This too shall pass, and all that." She paused to roll her shoulders and stretch. "I want you to sit there and imagine the best possible outcome. Sunshine, rainbows, big musical number, the works. I'll handle the rest."

"If you say so…"

"I do say so. Think happy thoughts, hon. That's an order."

I smiled at the casual endearment and recentered myself. As a master necromancer, I dealt in death and unsavory rituals that were the opposite of what Ivy was asking me to envision, so I focused on the idea of touring the country with Ivy and her band. I'd never taken the time to linger during travel—I wanted to get from point A to point B as fast and efficiently as possible. What would it be like to linger? To visit the states I usually flew over when traveling?

I imagined watching Ivy playfully bicker with her bandmates, the bonds between them as strong as though they'd been born as siblings—found family, Patience called it. Hearing Ivy's bright, brilliant laughter, seeing her clever smirk and warm smile. A future where she looked at me with trust and not fear.

A better future than I deserved. Men like me had no right to a fairy tale happy ending, but perhaps…

My thoughts wandered as Ivy worked, until Faust finally knocked and informed us that it was almost time to leave. I rose and perched on the edge of the bed.

"What do you need me to do during the ritual?"

"Defend me. The demons will know we're up to something, and they're going to want to stop it."

"The others will be defending you as well."

"I know. You're my last line of defense." Her lips twitched in a weak smile. "Might also need you to support me—literally and figuratively. If things get out of control a physical connection should ground me."

I smiled. "You want to hold hands?"

Ivy laughed. "I was thinking you could wrap your arms around me like an awkward prom pose. You know, I never went to prom. Dropped out too soon."

"I did."

"Let me guess, you were the prom king?"

"Guilty as charged." I grinned and she chuckled, but then her expression sobered.

"This spell is going to be a wild ride. The problem with my magic is that it's easy to be overwhelmed. Like that." She waved at the sleet pelting the windows. "It's a rush to call the storm, but it's a bitch to control it. That's how most tempests burned out. Consumed by magic. Very poetic."

"I've got you. I won't let that happen." I stood and held my hand out to help her rise. She set her guitar aside, wiped her palms on her jeans and took my hand. I pulled her into an embrace and held her tight. I closed my eyes and inhaled the scent of singed mint.

"It's going to work," I murmured.

"Right. Just need to give the performance of a lifetime. No pressure there."

"You've got this."

"*We've* got this." Ivy straightened and met my eyes. "Come on, handsome. Let's go save the world."

CHAPTER FOURTEEN

Ivy

The answer to how we were going to travel from Zach's tower to the place of power on Simon's property during the demon apocalypse was dragon transportation. I thought Faust was joking until we emerged from the stairwell onto the building's roof access and discovered an enormous scaled creature clinging to the structure like a B-movie monster while my conjured storm howled around us.

Shit. This was a terrible idea.

Apparently two dragons would be transporting the soul mate brigade to our destination—James and Thomas, who according to Patience and Faust had fought the demons/hunters last Fall at a shapeshifter gathering and were itching for another chance to stomp more demons into the ground.

I froze. "I don't think I can do this."

"Afraid of heights?" Patience asked.

One enormous yellow eye regarded me and then huffed a blast of steam. "I like your music."

My jaw dropped—the *dragon* was a Poison Apples fan.

"But your last album was too mainstream."

Patience threw her head back and cackled as I gaped at the enormous, scaled music critic. "You're not from *Rolling Stone*, are you?"

"That's quite enough, thank you," Faust said. "We are on a tight schedule."

I turned to Zach, expecting my soul mate to back me up, but he simply shrugged and hustled me toward the dubious safety of the saddles that would turn us into dragon riders.

"It'll make an amazing song." Zach picked me up and placed me in a saddle and I fought the urge to kick him.

"I hate you."

"No you don't." Zach buckled safety straps that lashed my waist and legs to the riding apparatus.

"I can't do this." My voice hitched a panicked octave.

Zach held my face in his hands. "You can. I'll be right behind you. Just hold on tight."

"It's not a fucking roller coaster. I'm not going to hold my hands up for the camera."

"James uses he/him pronouns." Patience hopped into the spot in front of me, and thankfully she doused her flaming wings before she set me on fire.

"He's not a roller coaster," I amended.

Zach kissed me and then took the spot behind me. Faust, Patience, Helen, Zach and I were riding one dragon, while Simon, Anne, Nati, Cris, Michael and Emily were taking the other. Nati and Cris had wanted to stick with Patience and Faust, but everyone agreed that Helen needed to be kept away from Michael and Emily, preferably at all times.

"Hang on tight!" James roared. He flapped his giant, leathery wings and launched himself into the storm.

I clung to the pommel of the saddle for dear life and

screamed, the sound lost in the rushing wind. My magic surged—we were part of the storm, among the clouds. Energy crackled between my fingers and zinged up my arms, and I hunched forward and fought the urge to connect with the storm. No point in burning out before my grand finale. Instead, I focused on panicking over the fact that I was strapped between the wings of a living, breathing air taxi. Beneath me I felt the rise and fall of the dragon's breath expanding and contracting his lungs. Freezing wind buffeted us as James navigated the storm, and I crouched low toward the heat that emanated from him.

Heat? Shouldn't dragons be cold blooded like lizards?

We emerged from the edges of the storm and sailed over the lights of the suburbs. The landscape was littered with fires—burning buildings and engulfed cars, alongside the glow of fire demons moving in packs that flowed in serpentine movements through the streets. I squeezed my eyes closed as my queasy stomach rolled. There was a reason why I spent so much time crossing the country in a tour bus, and that reason was because Paz and I hated flying. I'd dose myself with anti-nausea meds and suffer through it when absolutely necessary, but this was fucking terrifying and there wasn't a Dramamine large enough to save me.

An unholy screech split the rhythmic sound of beating wings, and I swear that the dragon cursed. I cracked my eyes open and spotted the outline of a nightmare creature, a misshapen void in the darkness like an inkblot test brought to life that was coming right toward us. It screeched again and the strident sound sent a chill down my spine and my jaw clenched.

Flying demons? This was *bullshit*.

James wheeled and answered the question of why the scaled beast felt warm when he breathed a gout of fire at the demon, bathing us in heat like a blast from an oven. I grimaced—of course flying demons and fire-breathing dragons were actual things. This opened a whole new terrifying world of source material for future songs. The demon howled another inhuman shriek, but then two more grating voices joined its chorus.

Three flying demons versus two dragons. I didn't like those odds, but I wasn't confident enough in my lightning control to try to fry one of them while in flight. I was just as likely to zap us or the second dragon. A demon dove at us and Patience produced a crossbow from gods knew where and opened fire. A bolt hit it square in the torso, but then we were blindsided as a second demon struck from behind. I ducked and covered as the dragon's head whipped around to snap at the demon attacking its back. The demon scrabbled for purchase and I yelped as pain slashed down my left leg, and then the world around me lurched to the side and I found myself airborne.

My terrified screams were lost to the wind as I plummeted. I was desperate to think of a spell, any spell, that would catch me, but panic scrambled my thoughts. Something tackled me and I gasped, my fall suddenly stopped. I blinked at the sight of black feathered wings, dark sunglasses and a familiar smile.

"I've got you." Faust grinned.

Holy shit—Faust had wings! Giant, badass dark angel wings worthy of song. I was so writing a ballad about him if we lived through this.

"Thanks. Your wings are stunning."

"Why thank you. My wife quite agrees."

"I love my new family," I blurted. Faust's expression softened.

"We're quite fond of you as well."

We zoomed back to the dragon just as James crunched a demon like a potato chip, and Thomas, the second dragon, batted another out of the sky like an enormous cat with a toy. I struck the third with a bolt of lighting, and after Faust and I got situated we were on our way again.

The dragons descended when we reached a forested area —an oasis of winter trees surrounded by urban sprawl. A lone house stood near the circle, presumably Simon's home, but I lost sight of it when we landed in a small clearing where the rest of Team Soul Mates gathered.

"Are you all right?" Zach asked. He kneeled beside me and examined the wound on my leg.

"Honestly I've been pumped with too much adrenaline to notice."

Zach grimaced and called for Catherine Duquesne. She swatted him away when she arrived and demanded that he let her work. I studied her as she chanted a healing spell over the long gash left by the demon.

"Shouldn't you be in a bunker somewhere?" I asked.

"Being pregnant didn't stop me from joining the sealing spell downtown."

"Yeah, but the ante's been upped considering the unholy horde rampaging through the streets."

Catherine shrugged and patted my healed leg. "Just means we can't fail."

Great. Like I needed more pressure. I fidgeted and lowered my voice. "Are we doing the right thing? The Faerie Council made it clear that they're not consenting to this. We're dragging an entire people out of their safe, secure home to deal with the racist shitshow that is humanity."

"The *right* thing?" She tilted her head. "Maybe not. The right thing would probably be to nobly accept our fates and go down fighting, but fuck that. I want to live."

I grinned. "Then let's get this party started."

The rest of my band were setting up their instruments in the center of the circle. I paused, hands on my hips. "I thought this was a solo gig."

Jorge snorted. "What, and let you get all the credit for saving the world?"

"More like letting me take all the blame. You don't have to do this."

"We know." Wolfie grinned and twirled his drumsticks.

I sighed with fond exasperation. "Thanks, guys. I set the spell to the melody for 'Bad Witch'. We keep playing it on a loop until it works or..."

I trailed off and they nodded. "It'll work," Paz said.

It had to.

Zach pulled me aside and held me close. "You can do this. I'll protect you. Everyone here is going to get you the time you need."

I nodded, my throat tight and raw. "I'm not a hero."

"You're a rock star, that's cooler than a hero."

I laughed and kissed him. "Thanks."

Helen approached me and held out her hands to take mine. I eyed her warily and reluctantly held her hands.

"Before we begin," she said, "you need to connect to the weave. Once you can sense it, you'll know how to begin unraveling it."

"Like a magic kitten with a ball of yarn, got it."

Helen laughed—she had the super villainess laugh down pat, and I saw Paz flinch out the corner of my eye. Lord and Lady, this was going to take the evil mother-in-law stereotype to all new levels.

"Close your eyes." She gently squeezed my hands. "Chant with me. *We are the flow, we are the ebb, we are the weavers, we are the web.*"

"Sounds like a witch spell," Jorge commented to Paz.

"It is," Paz said. "It's usually meant for coven bonding and group spells."

I ignored them, closed my eyes as instructed and chanted along with Helen. I was skeptical at first—I wasn't a witch, and my magic could be unpredictable. I focused on Helen's voice and the gentle cadence of the chant, and I began to see threads. Thin golden strands wafted through the darkness behind my closed eyes, and then they began to twist and dance as additional colors appeared. Some threads thickened into braids, others wound together like cables, and then they began to weave together.

Helen's chant slowed to a stop and I opened my eyes. The threads persisted as a ghostly image that underlaid my normal sight.

"Whoa." I reached out and gently ran my fingers over the shining bonds that connected me to Zach.

"Trippy, right?" Anne said.

"No kidding."

Zach frowned in concern and I waved him off with a smile. Helen squeezed my hands one last time and stepped back.

"Now you're ready." She grinned, and I nodded.

The band's setup was a combination of our standard gear powered and amplified by faerie shenanigans rather than standard speakers and electricity. I picked up my guitar, played a few test chords, and then stepped up to the mic.

"Ladies and gentlemen, Poison Apples would like to welcome you to the end of the world. We'll be performing music to demolish Faerie by, so strap in, stay safe, and remember, I am Ivy Taylor and my words are poison."

Wolfie howled and counted it out, "One, two, three, four!"

We launched into the song and I belted out the new,

"improved" lyrics. I was used to the rush of performing, and the spell formed around us in a slowly rising wave. I closed my eyes and envisioned the effect of the magic—my poisonous words were like acid, hissing and spitting as they wore away the weave that bound Faerie. I was destruction. I was the storm that leveled everything in its path.

I was attracting attention.

"Incoming," Patience yelled.

I opened my eyes just in time to see James and Thomas rear their scaly heads and stare west toward the road we'd flown over. The dragons had stayed to defend us—either they shared Portia and Faust's opinion that our world was worth saving, or they were just bored of being trapped in Faerie with the rest of the magical creatures kept there for their own safety.

I squeezed my eyes shut and focused entirely on the spell. The others would have to hold the line.

~

Zach

We arranged ourselves in a protective ring around the band, and Faust loaned me a long sword with the advice not to lose it because it was one of Patience's favorites. Thanks to my faerie relatives I'd trained with a ridiculous number of archaic weapons over the years, and a bladed weapon did make sense against the demons that would be drawn to the spell. I tested the balance of the weapon as Poison Apples started the spell, and true to form, a nearby group of demons was drawn to the magic. The bare branches of the winter trees scraped and snapped ominously as the dragons roared a battle cry.

"Armor would have been nice," I muttered.

"You're not used to fighting in armor," Faust said.

"You can have armor for the next apocalypse, nephew-in-law," Patience said.

"Thanks."

I drew on my inner fire magic and coated the blade with enchanted flames just as the first line broke from the trees. Shadow demons oozed forth and I charged the closest one. The monster hissed and bared its sharp, needle-like teeth. Not to be outdone, I bared my own fangs as I lunged and swung my blade. Banishing the demons would buy us little time since they could return quickly through the open portals, but every minute helped as Ivy's spell gained momentum.

"Go back to hell!" My sword slashed through the monster's chest and it collapsed into a puddle of sticky tar.

"On your left," Faust said.

I whirled to face my next target and time blurred as battle surged around us. I gained a collection of scrapes and bruises as I banished several demons, and then a demon tackled me from behind and drove me to the ground, knocking the sword from my grasp. Claws raked deep gouges down my back, shredding my cashmere coat and the shirt and skin beneath. I struggled to buck the demon off and it struck the back of my head. Spots danced in my field of vision and I faintly heard Faust call my name through the ringing in my ears.

The crushing weight vanished and I rolled to one side. A hellhound scrabbled in the dirt beside me and the tip of a silver spear exploded from the beast's chest. Banished, it disintegrated into a shower of ash and dying sparks. Alexander Duquesne extended a hand to help me up, and as I squinted at the sight and wondered if I'd been hit in the head harder than I thought.

"Come on," he drawled. "Up and at 'em, Harrison."

I took the offered hand and was pulled to my feet. "Thanks."

"Don't mention it." Duquesne thumped my shoulder amiably and I hissed in pain. "I've got your six."

I blinked in surprise but was thrown into the next battle before I could comment. Together we struggled to hold the line against endless waves of nightmare creatures, and despair hovered at the edge of my mind—no matter how many we banished, the demons would keep coming.

A scream pierced the chaos and was cut ominously short. Dread formed an icy knot in my stomach, but I refused to turn until I finished with the snarling problem I currently grappled with. When a second scream followed I finally turned toward it, drawn by the utter heartache in the sound. I caught a single glimpse of Emily Black cradling her husband's motionless body in her arms before a swarm of shadow demons descended like a feeding frenzy of sharks and blocked the pair from sight.

"No!" Simon moved to wade into the fray, but Faust and I grabbed his arms and dragged him back.

"They're gone," Faust said. "You can't help them."

"Protect Anne," I said.

"Reform the line." Marie Duquesne shouted the order from the other side of the circle, doubtless attempting to restrain her soul mate, Dr. Dannaher, from diving into the shadow swarm after his fallen mentor.

Simon struggled against us for a moment, hitched a sobbing breath and then returned to the battle. Faust and I shared a heavy glance before manning our posts once again.

~

Ivy

"Bad Witch" already was a song filled with rage and an urge to destroy—the patriarchy, in particular—so it meshed well with Helen's spell. As the spell built, so did my magic, and the wind picked up and howled through the trees as the battle raged around us. Demons shrieked and snarled and our defenders shouted warnings and barked orders. A heart-broken scream split the chaos behind me, but I couldn't stop to see what had happened—the spell was the ultimate example of how the show must go on. Our world depended on it.

The sound of breaking branches seemed to echo the snapping threads of the weave. Could the faeries feel the boundaries of their world fraying? Did the earth shake beneath them as we repeated each refrain? Would the councilors who had doomed us show up to stop us? The dragons could probably take them, or at least keep them occupied long enough for the boys and I to finish.

Speaking of dragons, the sound of rushing wings caught my attention and I looked up just in time to spot an enormous winged demon hurtling toward us.

"Get down!" I tackled Paz and shielded him as the dive-bombing demon missed us by a hair's breadth.

"What the fuck is that?" Paz asked.

"How should I know?"

Jorge pulled us both to our feet. "It's a night flyer."

"Not helpful." I dusted myself off while Wolfie kept the beat going on the drums.

"Keep playing," Patience called to us. She shot a crossbow bolt at the demon as it circled and it shrieked in pain.

Paz and Jorge took their places, but before I could start the spell again I hurled lightning at the flyer. The creature crashed into the forest and I took up my guitar. I'd barely managed the opening words when another flyer swooped out of the clouds and attacked. I dove for cover and heard a giant crash as Wolfie screamed.

I looked up and the drum set had been demolished. The flyer and Wolfie were tangled in a snarl of teeth and claws. Crossbow bolts zipped overhead and struck the flyer in the back, and then a spell grenade splashed over the creature. It shrieked and dissolved, leaving Wolfie behind in a crumpled heap.

"No!" I scrambled to his side and clutched Wolfie—I had zero healing skills and I frantically looked around for Catherine Duquesne. Wild magic didn't play well with other magic, but I had to do something.

"I'm sorry," Wolfie slurred.

"Hey, you're fine. It's gonna be all right."

"Okay." He smiled weakly, and then exhaled his last breath and died in my arms.

I stared, frozen in stunned silence as the world around me seemed to pause. This wasn't supposed to happen. We were supposed to be heroes and save the world. My boys couldn't die.

"Ivy!"

I looked up as my soul mate called my name and our eyes locked. Blood oozed down his face from a slash that angled from his forehead to his cheek and nearly gouged his eye.

We were losing. We were going to lose.

I threw back my head and screamed, pouring my rage, fear and anguish into the remnants of the spell until something shattered. Power surged and the storm blasted through me until I was certain that I would burst from the endless rush of magic. I was a creature composed of howling wind and stinging snow, just barely clinging to my body with shivering, frozen fingertips as my control slipped away.

~

Zach

Ivy screamed and I felt the moment that the barrier between our world and Faerie broke—and judging by the way our group staggered as though the ground shifted, they felt it as well. Magic rose around us in fits and waves and the storm that had been brewing unleashed its fury. *Power.* I'd never felt so much power, and it raced through my body like a rush of adrenaline. My wounds knit shut and I turned toward my soul mate.

The blizzard buffeted me as I struggled to reach Ivy's side. I pulled her away from her drummer's body and clutched her close

"I can't hold on." Ivy sobbed and struggled for breath.

"Yes, you can. You're amazing. You can do anything."

She shook her head and gasped for breath. "Gonna burn up."

I grimaced—if I was feeling a rush of power from Faerie's dissolution, Ivy had to be experiencing it as well, and it was affecting her already frayed control. If I drained the excess power she should be able to marshal her senses.

"I'm sorry for this. I love you."

I tilted her head and plunged my fangs into her scarred throat. She tensed and screamed, but I held her still as I drank her blood. Ivy's magic overpowered me, and I staggered as I was bombarded by the storm's rage. Damn it all—no wonder Ivy thought she was about to be consumed. No magician should be able to contain so much raw power, myself included. I was an alchemist and a necromancer, and I wasn't meant to channel this wild, untamed magic. It burned inside and out, as though I'd consumed a small sun.

I would burn so Ivy could live. I'd made so many terrible mistakes, committed so many crimes, and she deserved so much better than me.

I pulled back, overwhelmed, and screamed in agony as the world whited out around me.

CHAPTER FIFTEEN

Ivy

Waking up was a surprise, because I was pretty sure I was supposed to be dead. For a moment I wondered if this was the afterlife, but I was also pretty sure that the afterlife wasn't supposed to hurt like a bitch from Kansas dropped a whole house on me.

I cracked my eyes open and winced at the sight of Patience's face hovering an inch from mine.

"Good. You're not dead."

"Thanks?" I croaked.

"Not gonna lie, you tried extra hard to die on us. I have an all-new appreciation for whatever the fuck it is that you are." She moved away to perch on the edge of the bed—a hospital bed of some sort, though as my eyes focused and the details of the room swam into view the decor seemed too nice for the average hospital.

"Zach?" I winced—judging by how my throat felt like raw meat I'd definitely blown out my voice during the spell.

"Is fine. He's also recovering, because he's a dumbass like

you. No wonder you're soul mates." She handed me a cup of ice chips and I gently tipped a few into my mouth. "Lucky for both of you Cat Duquesne is kind of a badass at healing."

"Thanks." I made a mental note to send Cat flowers, or chocolates. "Who did we lose?"

"Don't worry about that now."

I slanted a dry look at her and she grimaced. "We lost your drummer, Wolfgang, which I'm sure you remember. And we lost Mr. and Mrs. Black. Simon and Anne aren't handling that well. Marie Duquesne lost most of her right arm but there's been some rumbling about faerie healers being able to grow it back. I'm trying not to think too hard about the mechanics of that."

"The faeries are speaking to us?"

Patience sighed. "Some are. Cecelia wants to scowl at you when you're ready."

"Sorry, not sorry."

"I know, right? They'll deal with it."

"Might as well get that over with, then I want to see Zach, my dogs and my ghosts, whoever's available first."

"Portia has your dogs—she's declared herself their auntie." Patience shrugged. "Whatever makes her happy. You have ghosts?"

"Anthony had them, last I checked."

"Ah. He's fine, so I assume he still has them. I'll check, and I'll go get the ice queen. Just rest."

I closed my eyes, and when I opened them again I was being glowered at by Cecelia of the Silver Crescent.

"You have no idea what you've done."

I quirked an eyebrow because I hurt too much to shrug. "Saved the world?

"*Your* world, at the expense of mine. You have doomed us all. The humans will hunt us just as they did before."

"You don't know that. Magicians just need the right PR people. I'll make some calls."

"Be serious," Cecelia snarled.

"I am being serious. I respect the power of social media." I fixed her with my own disappointed glare. "As long as we're alive we can work the problem. Like the saying goes, dying is easy, living is harder. We lost so many people—for centuries! —because we chose to hide instead of fight." I tried to fold my arms and quickly abandoned the gesture because it hurt like hell. "Did we seal off the hell realms?"

"No, not all of them." Her nose wrinkled as though the words tasted foul. "Even working together we didn't have the combined strength to seal all the pathways."

"Then I guess we're stuck with each other, aren't we?" I smiled, and she scoffed.

"I suppose we are."

"Great. Now, can we postpone the rest of the lecture until I don't feel like a dinosaur tap danced on my internal organs?"

The faerie vanished, and I took that as a yes.

Zach

After establishing that I was, in fact, still alive, I wanted nothing more than to sit at my soul mate's beside until she woke. I snarled at the first few people who tried to pry me away from Ivy, until my mother arrived and almost literally dragged me out of the room by my ear in order to deal with the motley crew of magical and non-magical authorities who arrived at my estate. Apparently our earlier rescue of wayward paparazzi had somehow set myself and Ivy up as some sort of experts on the apocalypse, and now local first-responders were asking for my advice on demon cleanup.

When I finally managed to break away, I learned that Ivy was awake and I hurried to her recovery room. She smiled when I entered, and I sat on the edge of her bed and took her hand.

"How are you feeling?" I asked.

She huffed a weak laugh. "Shredded, but alive. You?"

"About the same."

"Did you bite me?"

My shoulders slumped. "I did, and I'm sorry. I know I broke my word."

"You saved my life. I think that's an exception to the rule."

I raised her hand to my lips and kissed her knuckles. "Thank you."

"How did you know that would work?"

"I didn't." I lowered her hand and squeezed it. "I knew the magic was overwhelming you, and I wanted to siphon it away before you burned out."

Ivy quirked an eyebrow. "And you didn't think that it would burn you out instead?"

"Better me than you."

She tugged her hand free and lightly slapped my leg. "Jerk. You're lucky I'm too tired to kick your ass."

"Save it for next time we spar." I grinned and leaned forward to tuck a stray strand of green hair behind her ear. "I love you, Ivy. If sacrificing myself meant saving you, then it was worth it. I didn't want to survive if it meant being alone."

She sighed. "So. Much. Therapy. You're lucky I love you, too."

"Very lucky." I laughed and my heart felt lighter—we

survived. We were together and we could accomplish anything, therapy included. "Ready to start that redemption tour?"

Ivy grinned and her eyes sparkled with mischief. "Damn right I am. I'll order the T-shirts."

CHAPTER SIXTEEN

Ivy

Two Years Later

"This place is a real dive."

I snorted at Paz's horrified expression and patted his arm. "That's the point of a dive bar tour."

"Yeah, but..." He waved at the motley crowd who had gathered for the first stop on Poison Apples' triumphant return tour. An assortment of humans, magicians and faeries packed the cramped confines of the bar and spilled out into the street.

"I know. Great, right?" I grinned and he rolled his eyes. "I'll be in the green room."

The green room in question was in fact a corner of the basement with a card table and a couple of folding chairs. Zach was seated in one of the chairs, wearing his new honorary roadie uniform of jeans and a custom tour T-shirt that proudly proclaimed *My Soul Mate's Words are Poison*. He bounced his tiny cousin, Olivia, on his knee as the toddler drenched a werewolf plushie in drool.

I frowned at Patience. "You brought your baby to a bar?"

"It's a family event. We hardly ever get the whole gang together anymore." She shrugged and reached over to ruffle Olivia's bright red curls. "It's not like I bought her a beer."

Faust smirked beside her. "Good, because I'm not braving that line again. It's a madhouse up there."

I nodded. "We sold out in less than five minutes."

The knowledge was both affirming and terrifying, and I paused to take a few calming breaths. Recording the new album in the safe privacy of a studio was one thing, but this was the first time I'd be performing for an audience since the attack that scarred my throat. It wasn't hard to sell out a venue as small as this, but it was encouraging that people were excited about something as mundane as a concert—a sign that society was healing and embracing a new normal. The world had been irrevocably changed by the demon invasion, the return of faeries and the reveal that magicians walked among the straights. Borders were redrawn after ancestral faerie lands reappeared on Earth, and federal agencies were tearing their hair out over attempting to enforce travel regulations on people who could teleport.

I made the rounds and chatted with the friends and family gathered in the green room. Unlike Patience and Faust, Lex and Cat Duquesne had invested in a babysitter and left their son, Ben, at home. Anne and Marie had dragged their respective soul mates out of their libraries and were forcing Simon and Brian to be social, although "social" by vampire librarian standards appeared to involve discussing some recently unearthed text with Cris and Nati. I still hadn't managed to corner one of them to discuss the history of music and song in spellwork.

Riley and Jere were chatting with Wolfie's parents, who had made the trip in honor of his memory—Wolfie and the weretigers' involvement in canceling the apocalypse had gone a long way in improving the view of shapeshifters in magician society. Anthony had taken the night off from his new job as a magical law enforcement agent and brought the Gatsby ghosts with him. Jay and Jordan assured me that fighting magic crime was the cat's pajamas and both spirits were having the time of their unlives. They'd come a long way from communicating with me through knocking on the walls of my haunted mansion, but then again, I'd come a long way, too. It only took a soul mate and the threat of an impending apocalypse to drag me kicking and screaming back into civilization.

I returned to Zach's side, and he took my hand and laced our fingers together before tugging me down for a chaste kiss. "You ready for this?"

Warmth bloomed in my chest as he smiled, and I squeezed his hand.

"Yeah," I said. "I'm ready for anything. Let's get this show on the road."

ABOUT THE AUTHOR

Robyn Bachar writes romance with swords, sorcery and spaceships. Bachar's novels feature action and adventure, danger and suspense, found families and happily ever afters. Her books have finaled twice in the PRISM Contest for Published Authors, twice in the Passionate Plume Contest, and twice in the EPIC eBook Awards.

facebook.com/AuthorRobynBachar
x.com/RobynBachar
instagram.com/robynbachar
goodreads.com/iamtherobyn

BAD WITCH GLOSSARY

alchemist: a magician who specializes in brewing potions. The source of the magic is not the ingredients themselves—though they can help add an extra kick—but the alchemist who infuses her own magic into a potion. Alchemists are the most mercenary magicians because their magic is the most marketable.

chronicler: a librarian who has joined the Order of St. Jerome and become a vampire. Chroniclers undergo a ritual that was originally stolen from the necromancers and altered. It stops their aging and places the body in a sort of stasis. Like the original ritual, there is a chance of failure, and the odds of survival are only thirty to forty percent. To survive, chroniclers ingest magic by consuming the blood of living magicians and often take blood as payment for their services. Chroniclers are responsible for recording magician history and archiving spells and magical research. *See also* Order of St. Jerome.

Council of Three: a magician governing body. Every type of magician is monitored/ruled over by a Council of Three, as are faeries. There are levels to councils—regional, national, global, etc.

demon: an entity native to one of the hell realms. Unlike other magical creatures, demons cannot be killed, only banished back to their realm. However, if a magician travels to that realm, he or she can kill the demon there. Physical attacks on people in "haunted" houses are caused by demonic entities (ghosts can't physically interact with their surroundings). Demons come in a variety of shapes and sizes due to the difference in hells—some embody sins or vices, others natural elements like faeries, and some are just outright nightmarish bogeymen.

faerie: one of the magical races formerly native to Earth. Faeries are extremely long-lived, but are not immortal. In many ways they are embodiments of magic, the different clans representing different aspects and elements of it. Faeries left Earth and created their own world after the extinction of the elves, but that act left them damaged as a species, unable to reproduce with each other. A full-blooded faerie has not been born since the formation of their world. Many magicians owe their magic to their faerie heritage.

favor: a magical debt owed to a demon or summoner. Favors are no small matter, and are granted in exchange for powerful magic. A mark representing the favor is tattooed into the skin of the magician who owes it, and the mark disappears once the favor is repaid.

guardian: an enforcer of magical law and order. They work for the higher powers to ensure criminals are apprehended, but councils are responsible for judging guilt or innocence. Guardians can be called on to execute the guilty, if necessary.

hunter: an individual or group who hunts and kills magicians. Some hunters have personal reasons, such as having a family member killed by shapeshifters. Others do it for sport, believing magicians to be challenging prey.

kinslayer: a magician or magical being who has murdered a member of his/her family. Magicians have always been outnumbered by straights, and after the elves became extinct great importance was placed upon preserving the remaining races. Killing other magicians is frowned upon, but it is considered a great crime to kill a member of one's own family. Kinslayers are often socially ostracized by other magicians.

librarian: a magician specializing in history and research. Because they study a variety of magics, librarians can cast any type of spell. However, when a librarian casts them, these spells are less powerful. Example, a sorcerer's fireball is less like a softball and more like a golf ball if a librarian casts it. Most librarians aspire to serve the Order of St. Jerome. Though few are chosen to become chroniclers, many work as servants or assistants. *See also* chronicler; Order of St. Jerome.

magician: a person with magic in their blood. Most magicians have inherited their magic from faerie relatives, but in the past many humans were born with their own innate magic. This dwindled over time as magic faded from this world. Only people with magic in their blood can cast magic. No amount of equipment or materials will allow a straight to cast magic.

necromancer: a practitioner of death magic. Necromancers specialize in dealing with ghosts, zombies, and other icky dead things. When a magician becomes a necromancer he is apprenticed to a master, and once his training is complete he undergoes a ritual to become a master himself (*see* vampire). This ritual is risky, with a roughly fifty percent chance of failure. Master necros build up bad karma for jamming a spoke in the wheel of life, and when a master dies horrible things happen to his soul.

oathbreaker: a magician known to have broken an official oath. Sworn oaths are taken very seriously in magician society. If a person swears to do something, such as fulfill a quest or take on a sacred responsibility, failure to uphold the oath can result in social ostracism. Oathbreakers are considered untrustworthy, and few people agree to deal with them.

Oberon: an ambassador responsible for overseeing relations between Earth and Faerie (if the position is held by a woman, she is referred to as a *Titania*). An Oberon or Titania maintains balance between faerie and magician society within a region on Earth, ensuring that faeries do not cause too much mischief within that region, and that the local magicians do not abuse their access to Faerie.

Order of St. Jerome: the organization of chroniclers. The order was founded by a group who decided that having immortal librarians to protect magician records and be able to remember stories and events was necessary to maintain a record of magician history. The necromancers were furious that their ritual for creating immortality had been stolen, but a war between the two factions was prevented when the order agreed not to become involved in magician politics. The group has gone through many names over the years, but St. Jerome is the most recent and longest lasting.

seer: a magician who can read auras and receive prophetic visions. Seers are the rarest kind of magician, with only a handful in the entire world. Their visions center around the person they're reading or a traumatic event in an area. Seers are not mediums, and though they can get a feeling for the energy in a house, they don't communicate with the dead —because that's necromancer territory. Seers are particularly adept at locating a person's soul mate.

shadowspawn: a faerie who has been expelled from Faerie for evil acts. Though faeries have a high tolerance for mischief, they do have limits as to the sort of crimes allowed in and outside of Faerie. Faeries convicted of acts of great evil are expelled from Faerie, banished to live on Earth.

shadow realm: a hell dimension. The shadow realm exists in an eternal state of twilight, where the landscape, buildings and demon inhabitants are made of darkness. Vampires and shadowspawn faeries use the shadow realm as a shortcut to travel between places on Earth that are steeped in darkness. *See also* shadowspawn; shadowstep; vampire.

shadowstep: a method of transportation used by master necromancers, chroniclers and shadowspawn faeries. To keep vampires from causing mayhem in other worlds, the higher powers closed the doors to them— except for the hell dimensions. Shadowspawn faeries and vampires brave or foolish enough to make the trip can travel through the shadow realm.

shapeshifter: a magician infected with wild magic and possessing an animal spirit. The most common shifters are canine, with the rest made up of feline, ursine, equine and avian. Shifters coexist with their animal, almost like having a split personality, and can shift into a hybrid animal/human form and the full animal form. Many shifters, particularly predators, revel in their beast, which has led to shifters being considered subhuman by other magicians and even hunted by sorcerers. *See also* wild magic.

sorcerer: a magician specializing in elemental magic typically destructive in nature. Like witches, sorcerers use elemental magic, and tend to focus on one element in particular. In general their magic does not require spoken spells or physical ingredients; large, formal rituals are rare occurrences. Sorcerers are the magicians most likely to become necromancers, as well as being most likely to be kept as a necromancer's pet.

soul mate: a soul's perfect match. Soul mates are not always romantic partners and can be represented in other close relationships, such as best friends. Because souls are reincarnated, a person can meet his or her soul mate in several lives, or none at all. Also, due to free will soul mates are not guaranteed true love or a happily ever after. Seers can be helpful in finding a person's soul mate.

straights: a slang term for nonmagicians. There are many other terms, such as *voids*.

summoner: a magician dealing in summoning, binding, and/or banishing magical entities. Summoners capture and bind their prey, trading magical favors or power in exchange for release. They mainly deal in demons, but with the right information, such as a True Name, they can deal with any living entity—elementals, imps or faeries. Dealing with demons is risky business and wears on a summoner over time. They begin to take on demonic physical traits and may even become demons themselves, at which point they are often pulled into a hell dimension that becomes their new home.

Titania: an ambassador responsible for overseeing relations between Earth and Faerie (if the position is held by a man, he is referred to as an *Oberon*). An Oberon or Titania maintains balance between faerie and magician society within a region on Earth, ensuring that faeries do not cause too much mischief within that region, and that the local magicians do not abuse their access to Faerie.

True Name: the name of a magician or magical being that has power over that person. In modern society, names aren't given as much weight and a magician's True Name holds little to no power. It is considered rude to use a magician's True Name, especially without permission. The names of older beings, such as demons, faeries and vampires, can still hold power and be used against them. Faeries in particular guard their True Names jealously and go by a number of pseudonyms.

vampire: a slang term for a master necromancer or chronicler. *Vampire* is considered rude by many older master necros and chroniclers. They do, however, share some traits with the popular vampire myth. They must feed on the blood of living magicians—specifically on the magic within the blood—to maintain their existence. Most keep spouses, partners, or "pets" as blood sources. It is extremely rare for a vampire to kill during feeding (when you're done milking the cow, you don't slaughter it).

wild magic: a form of magic originating from an animal, known to be unpredictable. Most magicians consider shapeshifters to be *infected* with wild magic. This magic imbues its host with the spirit of the animal it originated from, and it also interferes with the host's original magic. Most magicians fear being infected with wild magic.

witch: a magician specializing in elemental magic, focused on healing and self-defense. Witches have a strict policy of doing no harm with their magic, which makes them unique among other magicians. Witches like ritual with their magic, using elaborate spells that require special tools, spoken words and physical ingredients.

OTHER TITLES BY ROBYN BACHAR

The Galactic Cold War Trilogy

Sci-Fi Romance

Firefly meets James Bond in this action-adventure romance set in an alternate future where the Cold War never ended...

Relaunch Mission

Contingency Plan

End Transmission

Bad Witch: The Emily Chronicles

Historical Paranormal Romance

Magic, matchmaking and murder!

The Importance of Being Emily

Poison in the Blood

Bad Witch Series

Paranormal Romance

Bad witches get things done.

Blood, Smoke and Mirrors

Bloodlines and Broomsticks

Bewitched, Blooded and Bewildered

Blood, Toil and Trouble

Fire in the Blood

Bad Blood

Blood, Book and Candle

The Bloody End

Just One Spell Series

Dark Fantasy Romance

Just one spell will change their fates.

The Sephra's Tear